Charles Mackay

The Twin Soul

Vol. 1

Charles Mackay

The Twin Soul
Vol. 1

ISBN/EAN: 9783337258344

Printed in Europe, USA, Canada, Australia, Japan

Cover: Foto ©Andreas Hilbeck / pixelio.de

More available books at **www.hansebooks.com**

OR,

THE STRANGE EXPERIENCES

OF

MR. RAMESES.

A Psychological and Realistic Romance.

IN TWO VOLUMES.

VOL. I

" Fay que mon âme à la tienne s'assemble,
Range nos cœurs et nos esprits ensemble,
L'amour l'entend ainsi ;
Tu es mon feu, je dois être ta flamme,
Et dois encor puisque je suis ton âme
Etre la mienne aussi ! "

—PHILIPPES DES PORTES. 1575.

LONDON :

WARD AND DOWNEY,

12, YORK STREET, COVENT GARDEN, W.C.

1887.

PRINTED BY
KELLY AND CO., GATE STREET, LINCOLN'S INN FIELDS, W.C., AND
MIDDLE MILL, KINGSTON-ON-THAMES.

CONTENTS OF VOLUME ONE.

THE TWIN SOUL.

THE TWIN SOUL.

A Psychological and Realistic Romance.

———◆———

CHAPTER I.

A RURAL HOME.

THOUGH I flatter myself that I am a philosopher, I am not a recluse. I love my books very dearly, as I do my flower-garden, my orchard, and my kail-yard, where, like the Emperor Diocletian, I grow very fine drum-head cabbages; but I also love at times to close my library door, to shut my garden gate, and go forth into the busy world, to mix with my fellows, hear their opinions and give them mine. On these occasions I endeavour to rub off the rust and mildew of rural solitude, to acquire, I will not say a polish, but a certain smoothness, from the lubrication of social intercourse. At the same time cultivate my sympathies by laughing at human nature, whenever, as Beaumarchais says, I am not inclined to weep for it. Some people call me a

cynic, others a wit and humourist, while a few consider me
to be a kindly and well-meaning philosopher, and speak of
me as the country people spoke of the poor gentleman in
Goldsmith's "Deserted Village," with a kind of wonder at
the vastness of my knowledge.   Others again, who are nothing if they are not critical, assert that I know too much
to know anything well, and say of me as the envious critic
said in another sense of the late Lord Brougham, that if I
knew a little of the world, I should know a little of everything.   But having a good income wholly unincumbered,
and being untroubled by reckless or extravagant connections or relatives, and possessing marginal money enough
to keep adding week by week and day by day to one of
the rarest libraries in England without depriving myself of
any other luxury, I manage to be happy enough without
caring very particularly what anybody thinks or says of me.
I am fifty years of age, a widower, and likely to remain so. I
was once in love, very desperately, with one who was as good
as she was beautiful, " but thereof came in the end" a short,
too short, happiness succeeded by " despondency and sad-
ness "—a sorrowful memory, and regrets for lost joy.   I am
to a certain extent selfish—all men are, or ought to be ;

for selfishness, like everything else in this world, is only bad in excess, like wine, or courage, or prudence, or a belief in the goodness of everybody. But, though I love myself tolerably well when I am in good health, which is pretty nearly always, I love my fellow creatures—especially when I do not see too much of them—and am glad if I can wisely distribute a portion of my wealth among the struggling and the deserving, to strengthen the weak, to lighten the sorrows of venerable age, or to help the young along the stony and thorny path that leads to fame or fortune.

I am fond of music and languages. I can play on the violin and the organ. I can speak French, German, Italian and Spanish; and understand Latin and Greek tolerably well; Celtic, Hebrew, and Sanscrit, less tolerably. I dabble a little in chemistry, have read all the writings of the old Alchemists and Rosicrucians; have made the religion, mythology, manners and history of Egypt, and of still more ancient nations, my particular study, and have come to the conclusion that I know little or nothing of any of them. I am not an Admirable Crichton; I can neither dance, sing, fence, ride, wrestle, fish nor shoot; and when I think of what I know and compare it with what I don't know, I am almost

—I will not say quite—convinced that I am a poor ignoramus, and that possibly I might pass the threshold of the great Temple of Isis at the age of three hundred, if I could live as long in mental and bodily health, and possess the same love of knowledge at the end that I do at the beginning.

I have a small house in London, a large one in the country, and my name is De Vere. I understood, when a child, that my father desired to call me Triptolemus, because of his great love for agriculture, and of his hope that I too would become an agriculturist. He relinquished his absurd idea of Triptolemus, for which I am very grateful, and called me Godfrey, after my grandfather. As regards the hope which he cherished, that I should become a great agriculturist and improver of stock, it has not been fulfilled. I cultivate no fields, only a garden, and, like the Roman Emperor, I live happier among my splendid "drum-heads"—the finest cabbages in the world—than I should be in the Senate, or on the vice-regal chair of Canada or India. No vice-regal chair would suit my caprice or my pleasure. I have a throne on which I sit comfortably—the great chair in my library—that stands opposite my writing-table. Here I am monarch of all the historians, philosophers, sages, wits, poets and famous story-tellers of all times. They are each and all of them my subjects, who administer to my pleasure and my instruction. They never "bore" me (I hate the word, but use it in default of a better), unless I happen to be in a lazy condition of mind or body, when I put them back on their shelves without offending them, to be ready for my use when I am more worthy of profiting by their perennial wisdom. In my library, placed on top of my book-cases, are six busts of great sages, all of comparatively modern origin, for I have no faith in the marble portraits of antiquity. Shakspeare the first, though I can't believe that the Stratford-on-Avon bust can resemble him; second, Geoffrey Chaucer; third, John Milton; fourth, George Gordon Byron; fifth, Walter Scott; and sixth, a poet in his way almost as great as any of them—Ludwig von Beethoven. Lastly, my inner study and private sanctum—my holy of holies, as I call it to the housekeeper, who would fain dust it and keep it in order, but is not allowed to do so, to her sore tribulation (I believe it is the only sorrow the good old woman has)—is adorned with two ancient sarcophagi from Egypt, each containing a mummy, as yet unrolled, but to be unrolled on some great occasion hereafter, in presence of a select and congenial few, capable of enjoying and appreciating the ceremony.

One word more about myself, when my personal revelations must cease. My income is five thousand pounds per annum. I state this fact, of which I am not in the least proud, in order that he or she who may be induced to read the following pages may look upon my writings with becoming respect, as not being the handiwork (or head-work) of a common fellow who writes for money, or of a mere man of genius who expects to live by his writings, and pay his butcher or his baker as punctually as if he were a banker.

CHAPTER II.

ONE day I received a letter from Paris from a particular friend, a member of the Academy and a chevalier of the Legion of Honour. The letter interested me greatly. Let me call the writer, for the purposes of this narrative, the Vicomte de Palliasse; that is not his name, but his family is as old as the first introduction of the palliasse into France, and it will suit him as well as any other. He informed me that he had given his friend, Mr. Rameses, a short but cordial letter of introduction to me, and expressing his confident belief that he was a gentleman whose acquaintance I should be glad to make. It was possible, he added, that the letter would not be personally presented for two or three weeks. Meanwhile, being of opinion that I ought to be fully prepared for the advent of a remarkable personage, he had resolved to communicate such particulars concerning ing him as he knew or had reason to believe were authentic.

Mr. Rameses, he went on to say, though he was sometimes called Ramsay, and which some people believed to be his

true name, was not a Scotsman.   He did not even believe
that he was a European, though there was a report that his
father or grandfather was either an Englishman or a Scotsman, who had been in the service of the old East India
Company, and that his mother was a powerful Begum, who
had been attracted by the good looks, stalwart presence or
flattering tongue of the Englishman or Scotsman aforesaid, and had contracted marriage with him.   He was
apparently about thirty years of age, was of commanding
stature and presence, had a jet-black beard, and a luxuriant
head of hair of the same colour, and looked as if he might
have sat for the model of an old Assyrian.   He was reputed to be exceedingly rich, and was certainly learned.
He had travelled in every part of the world between Co-
penhagen and Melbourne, and between Kamschatka and
New Zealand, spoke many languages, and was neither
Christian, Jew, Mahomedan, Buddhist nor Atheist, but appeared to be, as far as anybody could make out, a fire
worshipper—an ancient Druid, or possibly a Rosicrucian.
His manners were agreeable and his conversation full of
matter.   He was *tant soit peu* cynical, and such a favourite
of the ladies that the young men of Paris, the *copurchics*

especially, held him in detestation, and scores of handsome young women, who loved money more than matrimony—or who, at all events, behaved as if they did—had set their caps at him. But hitherto all their efforts had been in vain. "I anticipate," said M. de Palliasse, "that Mr. Rameses will create a sensation in London. All the ladies in Paris, mothers and daughters, desire much to know whether he is or ever has been married, but all who are impudent or imprudent enough to ask him the question receive such a reply, by word and look, as effectually prevents them from asking a second time. Probably it will be the same in London. Mr. Rameses has letters of introduction to a score of your dukes, marquises, earls, and other fashionable people and leaders of society. He banks with Rothschild, and is fabled to be a Crœsus. Anyhow, he is a very able and very handsome man, and seems, if I may believe his words, his looks, his gestures, to set more store upon the letter I have given him to you than to any of the others that have been showered upon him.

"His intention in visiting London is to study the manners, the customs, and the characteristics of the English, but I don't think he means to write a book. He has heard of your learning, and as he admires you, I suppose, on the principle of Boileau's saying : '*Chaque sot trouve toujours un plus grand sot qui l'admire*' (for 'sot' read 'sage'), you will admire *him*, and that you will both get on very well together.   Please introduce him to all the Oriental scholars, especially to the Egyptologists, but don't trust him alone with your mummies, lest he proceed to un-swaddle them.   He is very affable, and very good, but, as you will soon discover, he is somewhat eccentric.   But ec-centricity is nothing, or if it be anything it is a something that is rather agreeable than otherwise, if it be quiet and unaggressive.   So you know all about Mr. Rameses, or, at all events, as much as I can tell you.   I recommend him earnestly to your polite attention and amiable services."

It was not until nearly a month after the receipt of this letter, about which I had not thought much, that, sitting alone in my study in my small house in Park Lane— dingy in front, but beautiful enough behind, for the reason that my windows overlook the fair expanse of Hyde Park—that a well-appointed carriage drove up to my door, and that my servant brought me up a letter from M. de Palliasse, and the card of Mr. Rameses.   I hastened down to the reception-room, and found Mr. Rameses. He was staid, solemn, handsome, rather sad-looking, I thought. I gave him a cordial greeting. I had not been five minutes in his company before I was convinced that the commendations bestowed upon him by M. de Palliasse were not misplaced. The only thing that I did not admire about him was that his eyes were very black. I have a predilection, though the reader may think it wrong, for blue-grey eyes in man or woman, and somehow or other associate black eyes in men with an idea of ferocity. He spoke English as well as an Englishman—better than many who interlard their discourse with vulgar colloquialisms and the slang of the stable and the race-course—but he had a slight accent, which hinted rather than proved that he was a foreigner.

I had previously arranged to leave London on the morrow, and, without making any idle excuses, I informed Mr. Rameses of the fact, and I gave him, at the same time, a cordial invitation to visit me on a future day, at "The Rookery," to stay a week or ten days, or as long as he pleased.

"I have heard," he said, "of your mummies, and of the treasures of your library, both in manuscripts and printed books, and of your rolls of Egyptian papyri, baked tiles or slabs, and your cuneiform inscriptions. Can you read the papyri or the slabs ? "

" No, unfortunately. I wish I could."

" I can," said Mr. Rameses, "as easily as if they were French or English."

" Happy man ! " I thought, for my mouth watered at the information as the mouth of a hungry epicure waters when a rare dish steams before his nostrils. " Then," I said, " you will not pass a dull time in The Rookery, if you are as fond of ancient lore as I am."

" Dull ! " he replied ; " I am never dull. I am sometimes sad, sometimes weary with the world, with myself, or with Fate, Fortune, and Circumstance ; but I am never dull—unless, perhaps, at a fashionable evening party or dinner, when the gossip of fools goes bubbling up around me ; but even then, by a happy faculty of abstraction, my mind can wander away and go back ten thousand years into the scenes of a bygone civilization, or fly to the uttermost ends of the earth."

Here was a man after my own heart. I felt grateful to M. de Palliasse for introducing him, and doubly grateful to Mr. Rameses for condescending to make my acquaintance.

CHAPTER III.

THE ROOKERY.

LET me describe The Rookery. It is an old and spacious house (the guide-books call it a mansion). It was not built by any one architect, or at any one time, but grew like the British Constitution, and was the handiwork of many generations. The oldest part of it dates from early in the sixteenth century, and this oldest part, originally small, has received accretions at the hands of successive De Veres. Our original name was Brown, as I have heard, which we now write Browne, with a final *e*, and we took the name of De Vere on the marriage of the head of the family, a hundred and fifty years ago, or thereabouts, with a Miss De Vere, a wealthy heiress. Though of no order of architecture, but a combination of many styles, the old house is picturesque, and what is more, it is comfortable. It is approached by an avenue of elms, of half-a-mile in length, on the tops of which an ancient colony of rooks has long been established. Hence the name given to it by my ancestors.

In front is part of a moat, over which is a neat stone bridge, of antique fashion, that leads to the principal entrance. The moat, fed by a tiny spring of the purest water, is as clear as crystal, and is inhabited by a multitude of gold and silver fish, and by a profusion of water-lilies, that seem to me to be as full of life and enjoyment as the fish, and much more beautiful. The house contains three good reception-rooms, a stately entrance-hall, a picture-gallery, and my library—consisting of six rooms *en suite*. The grounds are extensive and well laid out, containing fruit, flower, and vegetable gardens (I am my own head gardener), together with lawns, shrubberies, and meadows, sloping to an artificial lake. There are, in addition, about one hundred and eighty acres of woodland, consisting of venerable yews, oaks, elms, birch, and beeches, and some very magnificent hawthorns, that began to spread their green leaves to the breeze and to the blast long before the days of the so-called " merry monarch."

I do not live alone at The Rookery, for I have a daughter —beautiful, good, affectionate, clever, the model of all female virtue and loveliness, the joy of my heart, the delight of my eyes, the mistress of my household, the belle of the county—who has scores of admirers, but not one whom she herself particularly admires. Her name is Laura ; her age is twenty-two. She is neither tall nor short ; she has splendid golden hair, perfect teeth, lustrous blue-grey eyes, a voice that is all music and melody, and when she sings, which she often does, not Patti herself could excel her —that is to say in my opinion—which may be wrong ; though I do not think it is. She has, I think, but one fault—she loves me too much, who am only her father, and proud of the relationship, and gives to me the kindness for a thousandth part of which more than one fine fellow in the county would be only too happy to marry her.

But at this period of my story, she is absent in Italy, with a friendly family, for the sake of a little change and recreation, which she needs ; so that the inhabitants of The Rookery at the time when Mr. Rameses came to visit me, were my mother, my sister, Lady De Glastonbury, and her husband, Sir Henry De Glastonbury, a man about ten years older than herself. They lived very much abroad, but when they came to England they always made The Rookery their home, and were always welcome. Then there was my second sister, Mrs. Brocklesby, the widow of a London merchant, who left her with three children and seventy thousand pounds. Mrs. Brocklesby usually passes the summer months with me in·the home of her childhood, for the sake of· old association, for love of the place, and for the fresh freedom of a country life which it affords her children.

When these visitors are with me, I meet my eldest sister and her husband and my second sister with her children at breakfast, and·see nothing of them afterwards until dinner-time. The intermediate ¡hours are spent by me in the library, into which, by an unwritten and unspoken, but well understood and implicitly obeyed law, no gossips or visitors are permitted to enter, unless by special invita-tion. When I am wearied with sitting, or studying, or otherwise ¡desirous of a change, I betake myself to the garden, and look after my flowers, my cabbages, and my gardeners, during which time I may be spoken to by any one who meets me accidentally and desires to exchange thoughts or words with me. My mother, kind soul, has one great grievance, the only drop of bitter in the otherwise pleasant cup of her existence, which is that I am a persistent widower, am not disposed to marry again, and do not cultivate the acquaintance of the young and beautiful, so as to give me the chance of falling in love with any one of them, or any one of them the chance of falling in love with me, either for the sake of worldly position, or as the French say, "*pour l'amour de mes beaux yeux.*"

She maintains that I am doing injustice to myself, to my country, to society, and to the long line of my ancestors, by not doing what I ought to do to become the ancestor of other people. To all her arguments I listen with patient resignation, and sometimes tell her that I am too old— which insinuation she vehemently resists as an imputation against herself—that I cannot fall in love by command, that I never saw but one sweet woman who approached my ideal of what a woman ought to be, and that she has gone and left no parallel; that if another of the same kind should cross my path, I would look at her, and admire her, but would not promise to fall in love with her; that I do not expect such a being is in existence, and that, all things considered, I am very happy as I am. "You are a fool, Godfrey," says my sister sometimes. "Call yourself old, indeed" (she is two years older than I am), "why, you are in the very prime of life, at the time when the blood is warmest,

and the reason strongest, and the imagination brightest !
One of these days, when you are really old, a quarter of a
century hence perhaps, you will be taken in by some
designing minx, who will marry you for your money and make
your life miserable ever afterwards, and serve you right !"
To this I seldom reply, except by the *pococurante* asser-
tion, that sufficient for the day is the evil thereof. But I
can see that my mother and sister believe all the same
that I am not so stony-hearted as I pretend to be, and that
some day or other, while yet in my prime, as they say, that
very wary bird, myself, will set his unsuspecting feet on the
bird-lime and become a captive.

These two ladies, though accustomed to defer to my
will, as the representative of the family, the inheritor of the
blood and fortune of the De Veres, were not altogether
pleased when they heard that Mr. Rameses was coming.
Not that they objected to the presence of a stranger ; on
the contrary, they liked the idea of a visitor. But Mr.
Rameses, according to the account I gave of him, was a
book-worm, a philosopher, a speaker of many languages, a
Rosicrucian, a Pagan, more or less infatuated with the acqui-
sition of dangerous and useless knowledge, a student of

antiquity, and altogether a person whose companionship was likely to confirm me in my bad habits of attempting to learn too much and make me more of a recluse and woman-shunner than I was already.   In vain I represented that I was not a woman-hater, but that on the contrary I loved and admired the whole sex, young and old, provided they were not scolds, slatterns or tipplers.   Lady De Glastonbury thought that a young man, such as she considered me to be, should not imagine that there could be women to whom such epithets could apply, and that those who boasted of admiring and loving the whole sex, did not in reality love anybody.   But I refrained from arguing this particular point, and endeavoured to persuade the ladies that Mr. Rameses was not a book-worm, as they imagined, but an experienced and highly-accomplished man of the world.

"But he is not a Christian!" suggested my mother.   "No but he may be as good a man, or better, than some who call themselves Christians," I replied.   "He is not to blame because geography and the accident of birth made him a sun-worshipper, and for my part I like the sun-worshippers.   They consider the sun the emblem of Divinity, and they worship the Divinity through the sun and beyond him:"

2*

"Idolatry!" said my sister. "But never mind, the poor man can't help his birth and education, and I shall do my best to make him comfortable, and, Oh! what a noble thing it would be if I could convert him to Christianity!"

"I hope you won't try," I replied, "for he might attempt, by way of *revanche*, as the French say, to convert you to sun-worship."

My sister smiled, for she is a sensible woman, and saw that there were two sides to the question. The result of my little rejoinder was that there was no further discussion on the subject of sun-worship.

When at the appointed day Mr. Rameses and his Persian valet arrived, my female folk did the honours of my household with a grace and a pleasantness that were very gratifying to me as well as to my guest.

It was evident that Mr. Rameses made a favourable impression both upon them and upon Sir Henry De Glastonbury. His noble, I might almost say majestic, presence, his sparkling black eyes, his dark, but not too dark, complexion, his faultless white teeth, that owed nothing to the dentist, his abundant hair, that owed nothing to the barber, graceful and well-formed hands, his small feet and high insteps, and the perfect ease and elegance of his manners, were all well calculated to impress the imagination of women. I never yet knew a woman who did not look to the hands and feet of a man, and dislike him if these portions of his mortal frame were large and ungainly. And then Mr. Rameses' deference to their sex, without servility or obsequiousness, or awkward attempts to please them by unmeaning and over-condescending flattery, suggested the gentleman — which he was — and put them as much at their ease with him as he was with them.

Binns, my butler, a man of venerable appearance, with beautiful white hair, a rosy face, and with an air of gravity that would have suited a bishop, looked somewhat askance, I thought, at the valet of Mr. Rameses, as Englishmen of his class generally do at foreigners, and Mrs. Grabb, the housekeeper, turned up her nose at him, not too demonstratively, in fact almost imperceptibly, but still in a manner sufficiently symptomatic of a latent dislike that was more likely to increase than to diminish. But of these matters I took little heed, being quite certain that when the day came for Mr. Rameses' departure, the "tips" or "vails," or whatever is the proper slang for gratuities, which he would bestow upon them, would reconcile them alike to himself and to his valet.

Thus Mr. Rameses was satisfactorily installed at The Rookery; and after a short rest, an ablution, and a lunch, he joined me by invitation in the inner sanctum of my library.

CHAPTER IV.

IN THE SANCTUM.

THERE is an electricity or magnetism (I was going to write freemasonry, but that is an artificial institution, whereas electricity is natural, spontaneous and irrepressible) between persons of congenial tastes and studies, which sometimes declares itself with the suddenness of the lightning flash, and this occurred between Mr. Rameses and me. We understood each other at the first interchange of looks, even before words gave expression to the ideas which prompted them.

"Excuse me," he said, "if I look at the backs of your books. I can never enter a library without an invincible curiosity to know what books are in it. Ah!" he added, "I see you have an imaginary library on the back of the door. Good! All the lost books of the Roman historians and the Greek poets! The original Homeric ballads! 'Eve upon Millinery,' and 'Adam upon the varieties of the Potato,' 'Nimrod upon the necessity of irrigating the plain of Shinar, and his purpose in building the Tower of Babel,' the nine books of the Sibyls, the reflections of Jonah in the Whale's Belly, the History of Human Folly, in one thousand volumes—volume the first, the nine hundred and ninety-nine unwritten! Ah, my friend, a thousand volumes would be all too few for·the mighty encyclopædia! But where are your Ninevite slabs?"

I pointed them out to him, and he was soon engrossed in the perusal of the first that came to his hand.

"I really think," he said, "that, for the preservation of history, the baked clay is better than the printed paper. If the great Library of Alexandria, burned by Caliph Omar, had contained nothing but baked tiles and slabs, some of its priceless treasures might have come down to the present day as certainly as the worthless thing I hold in my hand, which is but a mortgage deed on a house and garden."

"But not altogether worthless," I said, "because it proves that three thousand years ago there were mortgages on land and houses as there are now."

"Yes. Human nature, human wants, and human contrivances to satisfy them, and to discount to-morrow for the sake of the pleasures of to-day, are the same in all ages.

They were the same three thousand years ago as they were yesterday, as I can testify."

"As *you* can testify?" I said, with a slight upraising of my eyebrows.

"Yes, as *I* can testify. Do you believe in an Eternity with only one end? You and I are immortal—at least, our souls are—and if we are never to end, how can we ever have begun? The clothes and habiliments of my soul, after accompanying me and the earth in seventy or eighty gyrations round the sun, may wear out. But the wearer remains, and has to get new clothes, either in this world or in the next. And why not in this world?"

"Why not, indeed?" I replied. "But then, we do not obtain new clothes in this world—that is to say, new bodies after the old body is no longer capable of clothing the soul decently or comfortably; and it is of no use arguing or endeavouring to find out why not. It is sufficient to know the fact that we do not and cannot."

"But how do you know it to be a fact," asked Mr. Rameses, "that we do not, or that we cannot? I know for myself that this is not my first appearance in the world, though I most devoutly wish that it may be my last! You may not know and you may not believe when told that *this* fact is *my* particular fact, and that ,I know it and feel it as much as I know and feel that I am alive at this moment, and that I breathe and talk to you. And if you don't know it and won't believe it, the fault is yours, not mine, and my fact is to me an indubitable fact, in spite of your incredulity."

"Here," I thought to myself, as Mr. Rameses, his black eyes flashing phosphorescent light, thus delivered himself of his idea, "is the little eccentricity of which M. de Palliasse warned me." I never contradict eccentric people. I never argue with anybody whom I think to be more or less crotchetty—or, perhaps I should use a less offensive word, and say more or less the victim of hallucination—but, playing the part of Polonius to Hamlet, fool him to the top of his bent, and run no risk of making him furious by doubt, and, above all, by contradiction. So I carefully humoured Mr. Rameses in his idea.

"And on what do you ground your belief in this fact?" I enquired, "except what I suppose I must call your intuitive certainty that it *is* a fact?"

"By my imperfect remembrance," he replied, "of all that

happened to me in my previous dress or body, which I cas off more than three thousand years ago. I cast it off after having worn it for seventy years, and remained a naked soul, floating along in the atmosphere, until about thirty years ago, when I came into the world once more, bringing all my previously acquired knowledge along with me, dull and vague until my new adolescence, when it burst partially upon me. But we will not venture further upon the subject just now. At a future time, if you like to hear it, It will tell you the story of my first life—no, not my first, for I have led many lives—but the life before this, more than three thousand years ago, and will unfold to you the record of my hopes, my fears, my knowledge, my ignorance, my loves, my hates. Would it interest you, do you think?"

"It would interest me very powerfully indeed," I replied, still humouring him, and not venturing to cast even the shadow of a doubt upon anything he might choose to tell me; for human nature, even in its aberrations from the straight line, is always human nature to me, and there are wiser thoughts in mad people's brains than the world is willing to acknowledge. Not that Mr. Rameses was mad. No! He was not only a man of genius, but of common sense, which for all I know may be much the rarer quality of the two.

"Well," he said, taking a second slab from the heap, "another time, not now. It will be a long story, and may perhaps weary you."

I was going to reply that it would not weary me at all, when he suddenly exclaimed, as he passed his finger over the cuneiform characters, "You have a treasure here, Mr. De Vere! A contemporary record of the building of one of the Great Pyramids. Do you love money?"

"I do, and I don't. I have more than enough for my wants and my luxuries, more than enough for urgency, and for the maintenance of the old family prestige of those who are to come after me."

"That's good," said Mr. Rameses; "but if you really wanted or desired money, I would offer to buy the slab of you at your own price."

"If you will read and translate it for me, I will cheerfully make you a present of it, whatever its worth or its worthlessness."

"Worthlessness!" rejoined Mr. Rameses. "It would be cheap at any fabulous price you might mention. It clears up a historical doubt—no doubt to me, however. I will tell you all about it, and all about the building of the Great Pyramid, some other day. Meanwhile, I will not accept your gift. Bestow it upon the British Museum, or upon some similar institution in Paris, Berlin, Vienna, Brussels, St. Petersburg, lest it should be lost, injured, or destroyed in your private keeping. We will talk about it hereafter."

Mr. Rameses put back the tile in its place, and inspected another, with much apparent interest, but said nothing. He next proceeded to the papyri, several of which he un-rolled. "Nothing of much moment here. Records of battles and victories, renowned in their day, waged and won by kings whose very names have perished, and for the sake of the stability of Empires which are extinguished as completely, and have left as little mark behind them, as the soap-bubbles that children toss into the sunshine from the bowls of tobacco-pipes, and wonder at for half a minute Thus it has been with Egypt and Assyria. Thus it will be with France, Russia, England, America, and all the rest of the fussy nationalities, that think they are playing mightier parts in the world's great stage than ever were played before ! Let us take a walk in your grounds, Mr. De Vere. I want to get out of antiquity into the atmosphere of the living day, and feel the breath of the skies upon my cheek."

I led the way into the woodland, among the oaks and beeches, and was gratified to find that Mr. Rameses had as much admiration for noble old trees as I have myself, and that he looked upon them with the eyes of a poet and a painter. "Do you not think," he said, turning to me as we stood under the wide-spreading boughs of the very finest old beech in the park, "that men are a little arrogant in the pride of what they think their superior wisdom, but which may be nothing more than their superior conceit, in denying to trees and flowers the possession of a certain amount of intelligence ? The sense of enjoyment, accompanied as it must be, if it exists at all, by the sense of pain and suffering ? "

"I have often thought so," I replied, "as regards the trees—

" That all their leaves
In morns, or noons, or eves,
Or in the starry stillness of the night,
May look to Heaven in prayer,
Or bend to earth and share
Some joy of sense, some natural delight,
*   *   *   *
And feel through all their sap God's glory infinite."

" Exactly so," said Mr. Rameses. " It is the faculty of poetry to utter musical truth, and to say what we have all of us thought, but never found words to express The Greeks, who imagined that there were Dryads and Hamadryads in the trees, and Nereids in the water, were nearer to truth than modern mathematicians are willing to allow. And the ancient Phœnicians and the Egyptians, from whom the Greeks borrowed nearly everything they knew, were nearer to it still. Compared with the Phœnicians and Egyptians, the Greeks were only babes and sucklings."

" That would be considered rank heresy by most of the scholars of our day ; though I am quite prepared to accept it as indubitably true. But then my opinion is not worth much, as my knowledge is small, and I have not studied the learning of the ancient Egyptians half or a hundredth part as much as I should like to study it. And human life is short !"

"But I am an ancient Egyptian myself," said Mr. Rameses. "I have been initiated into their mysteries. I have been admitted into the Inner Circle, and I know, where others only suspect, Greece and Rome were but the great-grandchildren of Egypt and Phœnicia; and all the inventions and discoveries of your boasted modern civilization, are but accidental and imperfect re-discoveries of what was once familiar to me and my ancestors. But we must have a long evening alone to discuss these matters. At present I am weary of knowledge, and only wish to feel that I am alive, like a bird or a butterfly."

We talked no more about antiquity that day; but the more I saw of Mr. Rameses, and the oftener I conversed with him, the more I seemed to be convinced that his eccentricity was assumed—that he had a wonderfully capacious memory, in which he had stored a vast multitude of facts and ideas, all ranged in their proper niches, ready for use whenever he required them, for his own pleasure, or that of his listener.

We returned to The Rookery to dinner, where a few gentlemen of the neighbourhood assembled by special invitation to meet the distinguished traveller. Mr. Rameses made himself very agreeable, and my guests were all delighted with him. But after they had taken their departure, and we were seated alone in the " sanctum," he asked me as a particular favour not to invite him too often into company, and to be allowed, as long as he remained in my house, to dine alone, or with the family.

"You and I, and Sir Henry de Glastonbury, are quite sufficient company when the ladies have retired. English dinner-parties are only the feeding-times of tame beasts, and I don't care to be one of their number."

I was too much interested in him to thwart his wishes, and so I gave the promise of compliance, and kept it.

CHAPTER V.

A RAINY DAY.

"You don't hunt or shoot, Mr. Rameses?" said Sir Henry, at the breakfast-table next morning.

"No, I take no joy in killing. If animals are to be killed for my food—and I must say that I am almost a vegetarian, and eat little but fruit and grain—I like to have the killing done by an expert, by the poulterer, the butcher, or the fisherman."

"But don't you think that sport—I won't call it killing —is good for the health, and that it leads a man to take necessary exercise?"

"I don't," replied Mr. Rameses emphatically. "If a man desires exercise—as every man ought—he can take it without destroying the life of innocent creatures. Is it not as healthy to climb a mountain-top for the sake of climbing as to climb for the sake of the stags or the birds, and for the mere love of slaughter? I can understand the hunting of tigers, lions, wolves, and noxious animals, but I can't understand the killing of grouse, pheasants, partridges, deer, and other harmless creatures for the sake of killing them. Let the poulterers and butchers do it; not me! Why don't your ruthless sportsmen hire themselves out to the butchers, and kill oxen, sheep and pigs for the wages of the work and for the sake of killing them?"

"I am not much of a sportsman myself," replied Sir Henry, "and must say that my fancy lies in the direction of encouraging and improving life rather than in the direction of taking it away. If my health would allow me to live in England, I would cultivate my old taste—the breeding of cattle, and the improvement of the stock of all the domestic animals that are useful to mankind."

"Ah!" said Mr. Rameses, "that is a worthy pursuit. The horses—the cattle—the sheep of England are superior to those of every other country, and all because of the care taken to improve the stock—just as the pears and plums of France excel those of all other parts of Europe! It is my belief that the race of man is quite as improvable by culture as the race of horses—or of roses and apples."

"No doubt!" interposed I, "but you must remember that the horses, and the bulls, and the sheep, and the roses,

3*

are the slaves of man—and that man himself is free to indulge in vices and excesses, and to propagate his kind when he is drunk, insane or diseased !"

"Just so," replied Sir Henry, "and all ideas of improvement in the race of man, are idle as long as each man remains his own master. "What a blessing it would be if the diseased, the vicious, the deformed, the ugly, were prohibited from pairing, and left no successors."

"Aye! or could be controlled by the strong arm of a benevolent despotism," said Mr. Rameses. "The time was when this was done ! "

"When and where ? "—enquired I.

"In the days before history ! "

"If before history, how can you know?" asked Sir Henry.

From my own experience," replied Mr. Rameses. "I have seen it and known it."

"Cracked ? " suggested Sir Henry in a whisper to me—"off his head, as they say ? "

It had been raining persistently all the morning—and walking up to the window—opening it—and looking out—by way of changing the subject, which began to alarm

Sir Henry—but which did not alarm me, except for the fact that my sister just then entered the room, and might have heard what we were speaking about, I suggested that as nothing could be done out of doors we might profitably adjourn to my study. The suggestion was adopted. Mr. Rameses no sooner entered the sanctum than he recommenced the examination of the Babylonian slabs—some of which he affirmed to form portions of the historical books of the Kings of Babylon—venerable secrets of little use unless the whole record could be discovered.

"That is tantalizing," said I. "The world thirsts for knowledge, and it would be of the highest interest to the present and future generations to be able to reveal the mysteries of all but obliterated history."

"If you earnestly desire to pierce into the mysteries," replied Mr. Rameses, "you can learn to read for yourself the arrow-headed records, of which you possess so many; though it will possibly take a longer lifetime than you or any man can expect, to piece the fragments together—even if the·fragments exist. What a poor little mushroom thing history is! Soon grown—sooner perished—never completed! It is said that Truth endures for ever!

Bah! The Truth of history is unknown, but the Lies of history are imperishable!"

"Very true, and very sad," remarked Sir Henry. "But what's the good of complaining?"

"Yes; very true and very sad. But what's the good of anything? Except sleep! That is glorious, and would be divine if there were no awakening."

"You are too young, Mr. Rameses," said I, "to indulge in such gloomy, misanthropical, God-denying ideas as these. Life is good, and all the beautiful universe is full of it."

"Too young! did you say? I am miserably old! But I don't want to infect either of you with my melancholy. Don't call me young! I am old, very old! And the old-ness of my head drives the youngness out of my heart."

"Excuse the abruptness of the question, Mr. Rameses," said I; "but it relates to youthfulness of heart. I make bold to ask, were you ever in love?"

"Ever in love? I have been in love more deeply than I care to think of! I am in love now, with my twin soul —of whom I am in daily search, and whom I am compelled to seek all over the world, under the heavy penalty of daily misery, until I make her mine. Then I shall be happy; and then the end will come!"

"Cracked, very much cracked!" said Sir Henry in a whisper to me, as he prepared to leave the room. "Excuse me to him. I have a horror of people who are not quite sane. There is no knowing when the insanity will boil over!" And then, in a louder voice, he said, as he gazed for a few moments out of the window, "There is a break in the clouds. I shall take my usual ride after all. Will either of you accompany me?"

"You know," I replied, "that I never trust myself on horseback. Walking's the exercise that suits me best."

"It suits me too," said Mr. Rameses. "I love to think as I go, and if a man on horseback thinks about anything but his horse, he is very likely to come to mischief."

"Good-bye, then," said Sir Henry, "my ride shall be solitary."

Sir Henry left us, glad to escape from Mr. Rameses.

Left alone with me, putting aside a slab as he spoke, Mr. Rameses said, "I am afraid that I have startled Sir Henry, and that he has taken it into his head that I am not exactly in my right mind. He is welcome to think so if it pleases him, but I should not like you to share his opinion. I recognise in you a man in advance of his age, one who is not shocked at great ideas, even when they run counter to the preconceived opinions|of the world, as I wish to confide to you the history of my life and my mind. Will you accept the confidence?"

"I shall be highly honoured. The greatest joy of my life is to learn, and I feel that I can learn a hundred times more from you than you are likely to learn from me."

"Well," he replied, "the story will be the story of a soul, as well as of a body, and may possibly make you sad. Will you be ready to hear it if I begin to-night?"

"Quite ready, and all attention."

"Tell me, first—Are you a believer in what is called spiritualism?"

"A difficult question to answer. I believe in spirit or soul. And I believe that there is a sympathy—an attractive, an occult influence exercised by one living soul over another living soul in this world. I believe that friendship between man and man is a manifestation of spiritualism; and that love between man and woman, if it be pure love, of the soul as well as of the body, is the highest manifestation of spiritualism—you may call it electrcity if you will—that can exist in this world. But I do not believe that the living soul, that has departed from the body in this world, any longer exercises influence over a soul that still performs its own functions by means of its own temporary body. But this is not what the world calls spiritualism."

"No," said Mr. Rameses; "this is not spiritualism. Spiritualism affirms that the disembodied spirit is still an active power in our world of embodied spirits."

"I can't believe that," I replied. "All ghosts are of our own making, born out of a foolish or an excited imagination, and cannot turn tables, or write letters, or perform conjuring tricks. So if these performances, or others of a like nature, constitute spiritualism, I am not a spiritualist."

"I asked you the question for a reason. I do not, any more than you do, believe that spirit manifests itself in what is called spiritualism. But I believe (and I think I know) that spirit exerts itself in our living bodies with a power that is drawn from eternity, and that you and I, in this mortal life, are subject to the eternal experience of the spirit or soul that we hold for a time in the physical

embrace of our corporeal frame. Do you follow
me ? "

" I follow you, but do not clearly understand you."

" You are willing to understand—I gather that from all
you say ; and if so, you will understand my story when I
have told it you. The eternal nature of the soul, both
before and after this present life—that is my theme, that is
the secret of my history. To-night, if you will be a learner,
I shall be proud to be your teacher. But you, and you
only, are to be my listener. You will perhaps find that as
I am, and as I have been, you are also, and that your mind
will be opened, as mine has been, to many things of high
importance, that, as your poet Shakspeare says, 'Are
caviare to the million.' "

Though not quite satisfied that Mr. Rameses was not the
slave of a fancy, a hallucination, a crotchet, or whatever
else an aberration from the common-place may be called,
I was quite convinced that if he were mad, it was with the
madness of Hamlet, that his madness had much method
in it, that he knew a hawk from a heronshaw—when the
wind was in the proper quarter—and that I should derive
instruction more or less valuable, or, at all events, intellec-

tual recreation, from what he had to tell me. He expressed his desire to take a solitary ramble, so we each betook ourselves our several ways, and I awaited the night by taking a good half-day's work in my garden, among the flowers and the cabbages.

CHAPTER VI.

CONCERNING TWIN SOULS.

THE night that came did not bring Mr. Rameses along with it. But just as I was beginning to grow anxious on account of his non-appearance, little Jack Jonas, the son of one of my tenants, brought me a missive, written with a pencil on a scrap of paper torn out of a note-book, which informed me that the writer—Mr. Rameses—had been summoned to London on urgent business, that admitted of no delay, and that he would give me notification of his return. I wondered a little, not much, that his urgent business should have found him out in the neighbourhood of the Rookery, where he desired to remain unknown—but, as wonder was not of the slightest use, and no enlightenment could come of it, except by investigations and enquiries which I had no desire to make—I dismissed my wonder into the atmosphere, or into nonenity, if there be such a thing— which, *entre nous*, critical reader, is an impossibility. Anyhow, I speedily forgot all about Mr. Rameses, quite content to await his re-appearance to hear his promised story or his non-appearance, and speculated for a full half-hour or more on the singularity of his character, of on the doubtful point whether, like Hamlet, he was half-mad, wholly mad, or not mad at all. But I banished him from my mind as soon as possible, and buried myself, like a bee, deep in the petals of a book, from which I expected to draw wisdom, and from which I certainly drew amusement—a book by a living author, whom I shall not name, lest I should excite the ire of other living authors, who will never acknowledge an author to be great until he be dead and past rivalry.

I heard no more of Mr. Rameses for three weeks. After that interval he called upon me in Park Lane. My daughter had returned a few days previously from her Italian holiday, and was sitting with me in the study when his card was brought. She had heard all about him, and perhaps more than all, from Lady de Glastonbury, who was afflicted with an epistolary cacoethes, to a degree more than usually violent. My daughter was naturally anxious to see a man of whom she had heard so much; but, at the announcement of his name, she fled precipitately, giving the very feminine reason that she did not wish to appear before him in a deshabille that I thought showed her off to very great advantage, but which she declared made her look a "perfect fright." "Do invite him again to The Rookery," she said, as she imprinted a kiss upon my forehead, and drew her delicate taper fingers through my abundant hair (I have not the slightest tendency to baldness, having all my life avoided the use of tobacco), for I long to see him, after the description Aunt Margery has given me. Do, do, there's a dear !"

I promised compliance, as she glided like a sylph from the room just as the foot of Mr. Rameses was heard upon the stairs.

"You will have thought it strange," he said, after the customary salutations had been exchanged, "that I should have disappeared so suddenly from the quiet Rookery, in which I delight. I owe you an explanation. The truth is that I felt a malady, to which I am occasionally subject, coming upon me. On these rare occasions, I hate to be condoled with or pitied. What is more, I hate sick people, and myself most of all when I am in a state that threatens to make me burthensome and disagreeable to anybody. So I went away, and got well by myself, as I always do. I sometimes think that if I were a poor man and desired to gain a large income, I would become a physician, and cure all my patients (for large fees, be it understood) by doing nothing and prescribing nothing, and by no other course of treatment than that of putting on a pleasant face, and uttering a hopeful prophecy upon everything, and trusting to all bountiful and all beneficent Nature to work a cure. There is only one malady that cannot be cured by hope and wholesome inattention to it, and that is old age, the incurable disease, not to be scientifically described except by Anno Domini, or, as some would prefer it, Anno Mundi. And now that the shadow has passed over, I am come to invite myself once more to The Rookery, if you will tolerate me for awhile."

"For as long as you please. When will you come?"

"In a week, if that will suit you."

"Perfectly."

"During this week I have two or three invitations from great people in London, not very great to me, but great to themselves and to the outer world of common Londoners. I have accepted two of them, with a view of studying the manners of the English, I was going to say of amusing myself; but great gatherings do not amuse me, whether at dinners, evening parties, balls, or theatres. I go the day after to-morrow to the Earl of Stoney-Stratford's, who has three unmarried daughters;— lovely girls they say. I like to look at lovely girls, if they be sensible and modest and do not talk slang. Next day, a fascinating widow, of great popularity, greater ambition, and with a very small jointure, has made up a party, at an expense which I am afraid she cannot afford, to meet me— a poor, mysterious, unknown Asiatic, who is reputed to be fabulously rich. Shall I go?

"Why not? The proper study of mankind is man and woman. You may be amused."

"Possibly, though it takes a great deal to amuse me. My next invitation is from what in the slang of the day is called a professional beauty. I shall go, of course. 'Professional beauty' tickles my fancy; though a woman who gains notoriety, and loves it, by her charms, is not superior in my mind to a professional beauty, who turns her charms to profit and to pleasure in the harem of an Eastern potentate."

"You love the sex, you say, or, at all events, you like

them, and it is your object, being an idle man, not too much addicted to abstruse philosophy, to study them, 'pour vous distraire,' as the French would say."

"I neither hate nor love the sex. Why should I? I seek my twin soul, and I like to look upon lovely woman, in the hope of finding her. It may be to-morrow, it may be a thousand years hence, or it may be never! But why do I say never? There is no never! I shall find my counter-part soul some day. And then! Ah! then—what then? Happiness—great happiness, unspeakable happiness—ab-sorption, annihilation of self, and complete beatitude of spirit with spirit, never more to be associated with vile body."

"Vile body! Is not body as divine as soul?"

"Not quite. Is the violin on which you play as divine as the player? Is the eye superior to what it sees? Is the ear better than music? Is the tool superior to him who uses it? Is the perishable greater than the imperishable?"

The belief of Mr. Rameses in the twin soul was his craze, his hobby, his eccentricity. I will not call it his madness. After all, what did it signify? We are all mad, more or less, as has been said over and over again by wits, philosophers, and poets; and if I had asked my secret soul about it, and my secret soul had replied truthfully, as the soul always does, I should have been informed by my soul, that I too might be afflicted with one per cent. of insanity; that I live in a glass-house, and that I ought not to throw pebbles at the glass-house of Mr. Rameses.

"I see," continued he, noticing perhaps a slight shadow of doubt and perplexity on my face, "that you do not wholly share my ideas with regard to the twin soul that every man and woman in this world has to find, under heavy penalty—the penalty of being unhappy until the death of the body; unhappy, because soul and body are both incomplete until the meeting of the predestined pair, who, being a pair, are yet one. Too often they never meet. Hence the miserable marriages that are contracted every day by ill-assorted bodies, and still worse assorted souls; and hence the ill-favoured, imperfect, vicious and wicked children that come into the world that would be better without them."

"I do not see anything in your theory but a poetical dream, which, after all, means nothing but the necessity of sympathy in love and marriage. Without sympathy, love and true happiness are impossible."

"Very trite and old; excuse me for saying so," said Mr. Rameses. "Sympathy is common enough, just as antipathy is. There are many sympathies to enjoy in the world, and many antipathies to suffer; but there is only one twin soul for every man and woman. And the twin souls are fated to meet sooner or later. If not in youth, in age; if not in this stage of existence, in another; if not in this poor little planet, the earth, in some other and greater member of the sidereal system; if not in globular time, in infinite eternity. It is my fate to search for my twin soul, and I must continue the search till I either succeed or die —die in the body, to revive again in the soul elsewhere."

"I hope, Mr. Rameses," said I, "that when you look for the twin soul among the three daughters, for instance, of the Lord Stoney-Stratford, or at the house of the fascinating widow, or the professional beauty you speak of, you will not let them know what you are seeking, lest they should laugh."

"Well, if they laugh," replied Mr. Rameses, "I shall be spared the trouble of further search in their direction, as one who would laugh on so solemn a subject, cannot be my twin soul. Nevertheless, I shall not explain my philosophy to any woman whatever, or to any man, or any cynical

4*

derider of mysteries ; and if I have explained it to you, it is because I think you are really a searcher after wisdom, and that you do not despise theories merely because they may appear to be extravagant, or because the densely respectable, and the still more densely stupid, people who boast of what they call their ' common-sense,' may agree to laugh at them.   But I will not attempt to discuss the matter just now, or inflict my theories upon you in a hasty visit, when your mind may be pre-occupied.   When we are alone together at The Rookery, amid your books, with the mummy in the corner, and we have exhausted the subject of the weather, and of the dreary politics of your nation—politics that savour more of the narrow-mindedness of a parish than of the broader interests of the wide world, of which that parish is but a small part—we may indulge in speculations on the unseen and the unknown.   Such speculations, I must confess, have a singular fascination for my mind."

"And for mine too, if not carried to excess.   I sometimes think, when I am tempted to let my imagination run away with my experience, that I am about as foolish as a gold-fish, imprisoned in a vase of water (to him and his comrades in captivity the only known world) would be if he were to launch out into speculations about my library, about my country, about Europe, Asia, and America, or about the sun and the moon. Or, again, I often think that I am even more presumptuous in attempting to fathom infinitude and eternity than the animalcule in a drop of water would be, if he thought he were a philosopher or a metaphysician, a positivist or a Comtist, and began to speculate on the scheme of the Universe."

" The reflection is natural," said Mr. Rameses ; "but suppose an animalcule, that has escaped from the drop of water, or a fish that has been liberated from the glass vase, and seen the world ! *I* am that animalcule ! *I* am that fish ! I have been privileged to pass the boundaries. I have seen, and I have known."

" Ah ! my friend," said I, "seeing is nothing. The eye is the greatest of deceivers. I have seen much, but I know nothing. To see is not necessarily to understand or to know. I have seen the moon, and the stars, but what do I know about them ? Nothing ! nothing ! nothing !"

As we thus spoke, a letter, brought by special messenger, was delivered to me by my serving-maid, for I have no man-servant in the house, only a butler and a coachman, who confine themselves, by my express desire, to their own special business. I prefer neat-handed Phillises in my household to men-servants. The missive conveyed an invitation to myself and Miss De Vere from Lord Stoney-Stratford to meet Mr. Rameses. Though the notice was short, I at once decided on accepting the invitation, to the apparent joy of my visitor, to whom I handed the letter.

" I hope I shall sit next to you at the dinner-table," he said; " I hate to be placed with a fair fool, or with a silent, a solemn, or an unknown man, on either side of me, with neither of whom I can converse, except about the weather, for fear if I talked on any other subject, I might tread on the theological, the political, the artistic, or perhaps the social coat-tails of my neighbour. Why, in the name of all that is wonderful, are large dinner-parties given to bring people together who may not have a single feeling in common ? I like a dinner-party, not exceeding eight or nine people of both sexes, who know what to talk about, and who can accompany, by intellectual intercourse, the vulgar pleasure, or rather the *necessity*, of eating and drinking. I would as soon be a pig, and eat swill out of a trough, as eat my dinner without the civilising sauce of intellectual conversation. If I cannot find other society at dinner, I will dine with a book, with the wisdom, the wit, or the poetry of which I can sympathise, and in which, if I do not altogether sympathise, I can find something or other to stir my thought by suggestion."

"My soul," said I, "is twin with yours as far as that idea is concerned."

And with this remark our conversation ended.

CHAPTER VII.

THE STONEY-STRATFORD FAMILY.

THE Earl of Stoney-Stratford was an old acquaintance of mine, an accomplished man—a good man after his kind—and one that many, if not most, people would have envied, and with whom they would have been glad to exchange destinies—even if they had known of two little skeletons which he had in his cupboard. The skeletons were not very frightful, and ninety-nine people out of a hundred would not have considered them skeletons at all—or if they did, would have quietly locked the door upon them, or bricked it up hermetically. Skeleton the first was the complaint against Fate and Nature that had denied him a son, to whom he might transmit his title. He had, it is true, a son—who was not a son, in the eyes of the law—and of whom Lady Stoney-Stratford knew nothing, while the most ardent wish of his life was the possession of a son in whom Lady Stoney-Stratford should have as much right as himself. He had seven daughters, it is true, but in his eyes, much as he loved and admired them—for they were comely, and even beautiful—a son would have been better than them all.

The other skeleton was an unappeasable greed for other men's acres, contiguous to his own ; acres of which he could not dispossess the owners, even by purchase at three times their value. Why he so coveted these acres—some of them barren, or scantily productive—was a mystery to all sensible people; but Lord Stoney-Stratford loved to accumulate acres for the sake of the acres—as some men love to accumulate books, pictures, snuff-boxes, walking-sticks, or old china ; not for any good that these may yield to their owners, but for the mere sake of possessing them. Had he owned the acres, he might have been unhappy—but not owning the acres he was miserable, and life seemed to him scarcely tolerable. What was his title to him—what were his other acres—as long as the obstinate Jones and the equally obstinate Smith possessed the outlying fields, and would not or could not sell them ? And why could he not buy a field as easily as he could buy a ship, a bale of cotton, or a leg of mutton ? But he kept his griefs to himself as the Spartan boys kept their foxes—under their waistcoats,

defying the world to disbutton them and let out the prohibited animals.

According to public Rumour, who is the greatest of all
possible liars, Lord Stoney-Stratford's affairs were in
some embarrassment. " How," asked Rumour, " could it be
otherwise—when he borrowed money at ten and sometimes twelve or fifteen per cent. from usurers, to invest in
land that only paid him three per cent. ? " How, indeed,
supposing that Rumour for once spoke truth.   He who
scorns arithmetic, be he lord or ploughman, man of genius
or simpleton, must come to grief, if he lives long enough to
allow fate to work out the dreadful problem of income and
expenditure, when they are in disagreement.

Lord Stoney-Stratford's daughters were very costly
articles—very beautiful, no doubt, and they knew it.
Their tastes were very expensive, and if matrimony could
provide the means for indulgence in them, they were not
particular as to the age, height, health, character, colour
or other personal condition of the matrimonial partner—
provided always that the prejudices or opinions of Society
were not too flagrantly outraged.   They were not at all
romantic, though they loved romance in other people—

especially in the novels of women who scribble out
of the gushing superabundance of their ignorance of life
and of the rules of English composition—but for neither of
them was love in a cottage a consummation to be looked
upon except with contemptuous disfavour or positive
repugnance.   Lady Stoney-Stratford was an excellent
manager, where her daughters were concerned, and had
succeeded in getting four of them off his Lordship's hands
and her own.   She had married two of them to comparatively small fortunes and a title, and another two of them
for much money and no title.   Neither she nor her husband
had cared to build upon other foundations than these ;
though both were equally anxious that their daughters
should live respectably and not offend Mrs. Grundy.   The
dinner to meet Mr. Rameses was entirely due to her
ladyship's good management.   Mr. Rameses was more or
less the hero of the London season—was indubitably handsome, and was almost indubitably rich.   In addition to these
advantages there was a halo of romance and mystery about
him, which would not have encircled him with so much lustre
if he had been an Englishman, but which, being a grand
Asiatic, with a mixture of Scotch blood in his veins—who

might have had half a dozen wives in his time and whom he might have subjected to the bowstring, or the sack, or the scimitar—was of a nature to dazzle the eyes even to blindness of all the young lady devotees at the holy—super-holy—ever-holy shrine of the ineffable St. Mammon.

The Earl knew all his wife's manœuvres and sympathised in their object. If Maud, Ethel, or Gwendoline succeeded in being well married, and ceased to be a burthen on his resources, he might purchase a few more acres within sight of the windows of Stoney Court. It was reported that Mr. Rameses was a Parsee, a Jew, a Mahometan, a Buddhist, or worse—but what did it signify, if the marriage could be brought about with the consent of all parties? Maud, Ethel or Gwendoline, might become a Parsee or anything else if there were a million of money behind; and perhaps Mr. Rameses himself was about as much of a Christian as other people in England; and might embrace the faith to gain a wife after his fancy. "What will not woman when she loves?" asks the old song. What will not man do when he lusts?—might be asked with equal propriety.

There was a large party that night at the Earl of Stoney-Stratford's. There were several ladies, including dowagers and comely married women, among the guests; but there were only four unmarried ones—the three Pierrepoints, daughters of the Earl, and Laura Brown De Vere, my daughter. Laura was invited on the suggestion of Lady Stoney-Stratford—who saw deep into social things and social folks—who had an idea in her diplomatic head, that if no young marriageable ladies but her own daughters were present, the ill-natured critics and criticasters might whisper and hint, louder than if they blew a bassoon, a bagpipe, or ten thousand trumpets, that the party had been arranged with no other purpose than to ensnare the millionaire into a marriage with one (no matter which) of the blooming Pierrepoints.

Mr. Rameses that evening made himself even more than usually agreeable, and adapted his conversation more to the supposed tastes of the ladies than to those of the gentlemen of the party. He was especially cordial in his manner to Lady Stoney-Stratford, which he certainly would not have been if he had suspected the real motive of her diplomacy. But the suspicion never entered his mind. All the ladies were fascinated by his manner. He was modest and unobtrusive, but not shy. He was handsome, and did not appear to be aware of the fact. He was eloquent, but did not talk too much, and showed no tendency to monopolise the conversation, or to thrust himself unduly forward. A slight shade passed over his face as Lady Gwendoline, the handsomest of the three daughters of her host, used the words "awfully jolly!" But it speedily passed away, to return, however, a few moments afterwards, when she declared that something or other was a "horrid bore." It was evident, from the expression which flashed into his eyes, that Mr. Rameses, even if he had been in search of the twin soul, would not have looked for it in Lady Gwendoline's direction.

After the ladies had retired, the conversation among the gentlemen happened to turn upon the scientific discoveries of the present time—notably upon the uses to which it was possible to turn the mysterious powers of electricity. On this point Lord Stoney-Stratford expressed his opinion that this age was far in advance of every other since the creation of the world, and that society was yet on the threshold of newer and still more important discoveries.

Mr. Rameses dissented. "I have studied this subject," he said, "with a care and a profundity that I am positive— all but positive—that no man living, whoever he may be,

has devoted to it, because I have had unrivalled oppor-
tunities. It is too much the fashion in the nineteenth
century of the Christian era to look upon this particular
century as the culmination of scientific wisdom. Ignorant
conceit ! The ancients knew far more than the moderns,
though they did not spread their knowledge abroad, or proclaim it by sound of trumpets, and gabble of newspapers,
in the highways and the by-ways. The grandest of modern
discoveries are but re-discoveries of facts and principles
known—not for the first time nineteen hundred years
after the starting-point of the Christian era, but two or
three thousand years before it."

" But," interposed the Honourable Augustus Smithers—
a portly man with a very bald head, and a very pompous
manner—" are we not in advance of the ancients, say in the
matter of railways and steam engines ? "

" We travel faster than the ancients, undoubtedly," said
Mr. Rameses ; "a fact in which I see no particular advantage ; but the contrary. I see no good in fast travelling or
in fast living. Does fast travelling increase the world's
happiness, or that of the individual ? "

" Perhaps not," said Lord Stoney-Stratford. " The good

old coach and four was good enough for me, and for any body who could afford the expense. For those who could not afford it there was a choice of two pleasures, neither of them to be despised—that of walking or of staying at home. The last perhaps was the greater of the two."

"There is much to be said on both sides," said Mr. Bangles, a Queen's counsel and a member of Parliament, who was accustomed professionally to look at both sides of every possible question. "The great good that I see in railways and steam engines arises from the fact that they enable all the nations of the world to become acquainted with each other; and from the smaller or less important fact that in our day cities have a tendency to grow too large— much too large—for health, comfort, and amenity, and that railways enable people now and then to get out of them into the fresh air of the country."

"It is a large subject," replied Mr. Rameses; "but a dinner-table is not precisely the forum for its discussion, especially when the ladies are making music upstairs. inviting us to join them. Sweet music is better than argumentation."

"Let us rejoin the ladies," said Lord Stoney-Stratford,

passing the bottle to Mr. Rameses—who refrained from filling his glass—and then, rising, led the way to the drawing-room.

The ladies Maud and Ethel Pierrepoint were playing a duet from Mendelssohn as the gentlemen entered. "Do you greatly enjoy music, Mr. Rameses?" asked Lady Stoney-Stratford, with a more than usually gracious smile to the millionaire, after he had been listening for a few minutes.

"More than I can tell," he answered. "Beethoven more especially awakens feelings, memories, and mysteries in me which I cannot describe or account for, and which seem to me to speak a language without words—'Lieder ohne worte,' as he expresses it—more full of meanings than any language that ever was spoken. But you will, perhaps, think me eccentric if I say that the simple melodies of Scotland and Ireland have a very great charm for me, and exercise a power over my sympathies which is unaccountable to me. I sometimes think as I have some Scottish blood in my veins which I have inherited from a remote ancestor that my mysterious and occult love for Scottish music becomes explicable. Do the Ladies Pierrepoint play or sing Scottish music?"

"I am afraid not," said Lady Stoney-Stratford; "they prefer operatic airs—Italian, German, or French. We think in England that English, Scotch, Irish and Welsh music is rococo, vulgar; much too '*tuny*,' as we say."

"*Tuny?*" said Mr. Rameses. "I never heard the word before; but shall make a note of it. Tuny! Music that is not 'tuny' is not to my taste. But can Miss De Vere, do you think, not sing a Scotch melody, let me call it a *tune*, in spite of your Ladyship's disapprobation. Mr. De Vere," he said to me, who had overheard the little colloquy, "does your daughter admire Scotch music?"

"She loves it," I replied; "and is no mean proficient either upon the instrument or with the voice. She is one of those true singers, who do not need to be asked twice, but who sing as the birds do, because singing is natural to them."

Laura consented immediately, with all the grace in the world. I could not help thinking that Lady Stoney-Stratford looked displeased at her cheerful willingness, as if she thought a wrong was done to her three daughters by the fact that any other young girl could do what they could not.

" Shall I sing a sad song or a merry one ? " asked Laura.

" Oh, a sad song—a melancholy song by all means," replied Mr. Rameses. " The Flowers of the Forest," or " Lochaber No More." To me there is a charm which defies analysis, in plaintive memories, in the minor key—

> ' Gay music makes me sad—so prithee, sweet,
> Sing me a doleful, melancholy song,
> Such as Ophelia, crazed, and scattering flowers,
> Sings in the play ! '

And she sang " The Flowers of the Forest," and " Lochaber No More," the melancholy wail of despondent patriotism, to the great delight of Mr. Rameses.

" These, I suppose, are Highland or Gaelic, and not Lowland Scotch, melodies ? " said he to me, and also to Laura.

" The ' Flowers of the Forest' is a purely Highland air," I replied, "and is full of the peculiar pathos of the love songs of the Gael. I do not know whether ' Ye Banks and Braes ' is Highland or Lowland."

" It is neither, papa," said Laura ; "but French, adopted and improved upon by the Scotch, and very likely was introduced into Scotland or composed by Châtelard, the unhappy admirer of Queen Mary."

5*

"Would you kindly oblige me with another Scottish song?" said Mr. Rameses. "I cannot explain to you or to myself the singular effect which such music has on my feelings. It breathes to me of the long, long ago, and sends me, as it were, up the stream of Time, as if I had first heard the sad and tender melodies thousands of years ago!"

Laura, though surprised at the mention of thousands of years, only thought it an exaggeration of musical enthusiasm, and at once consented. She was running over the prelude to the livelier air of the Jacobite song of Prince Charlie's welcome to Skye, when the pompous Mr. Smithers asked of the still more pompous Mr. Bangles, Q.C., what the young lady was singing so much for?

"Don't you know?" said Bangles, putting his glass to his eye with an impudent sneer. "She's singing for the million —*à la* Hullah!"

The observation did not reach the ears of Mr. Rameses, but it reached mine, and those of the hostess.

Lady Stoney-Stratford smiled, as if she highly enjoyed the impertinence, while I experienced all over my frame a feeling of contempt for Mr. Bangles. The word *snob* dwelt unspoken on my lips, as I surveyed him from head to foot in a manner which the French designate by the verb *toiser*, an expression for which the English have no exact equivalent.

That my lovely and pure-minded girl should be suspected even by a "snob" or a "cad" of displaying her gifts to please Mr. Rameses, or anybody else, for his money, was an offence to my delicacy and an insult to my daughter, meriting contempt, which I was glad to inflict upon Bangles, and which I extended in a minor degree to Lady Stoney-Stratford herself, for seeming to approve of it.

The Ladies Gwendoline, Maud and Ethel were more or less out of humour with Laura's performance, but when I asked Lady Gwendoline if she would sing an Italian or a German air, she replied, "Oh, yes ! I hate Scotch music— but, no, I don't hate it, I don't understand it. It is so awfully slow and old-fashioned—quite too entirely gone by. Would you like to hear *Ciascun lo dice, Ciascun lo sa !* from 'La Figlia del Reggimento'? I think I could manage it."

"Oh, do !" said I, "it is awfully good ; quite too tremendously beautiful, in fact."

The Lady Gwendoline saw no mockery either in my

words or on my face, and she sang it "quite too awfully badly," though apparently to the satisfaction of Smithers and Bangles, Q.C.   These two were marked in the demonstration of their very quiet and restrained applause. Mr. Rameses made no sign, except in a faint *sotto voce* to me, "This is but shadow; the singing of your daughter is sunlight, moonlight, starlight.   I like a song with a heart in it, though my heart, I am afraid, is very much like an extinct volcano."

"You have more heart, Mr. Rameses, than you care to acknowledge," said I.   "All men of any culture now and then affect a cynicism which they do not feel.   It acts upon their system, you see, like sauce to fish, or mustard to beef.   I like cynicism if it be gracefully put on—like a mask, like a domino, as it were, with bright eyes and good features underneath it—unseen of the uninitiated."

"If anything," replied Mr. Rameses, "could convert the shadow of my cynicism into the substance it would be the Stoney-Stratford family."

"Then the twin soul is not to be sought in that direction?"

"The thought of the twin soul never enters my mind of

my own free will. It always comes unbidden, like a lightning flash—a divine prompting—a heavenly inspiration —and vanishes as suddenly, leaving its own memory and my regrets behind it—perhaps not reappearing for a space of time that seems to me to be centuries, though they are only the hours and days of ordinary mortals."

The attentions lavished upon Mr. Rameses by his aristocratic entertainers seemed at first to weary, and finally to distress him. He was the first to take his departure, and I and Laura followed after an interval of about a quarter of an hour, during which his merits (no demerits were even so much as suggested) were freely discussed by the ladies of the company, with an occasional word thrown in by the gentlemen.

" Do you not think, Jocelyn," said Lady Stoney-Stratford to her husband, " that there is a singular beauty in his melancholy face ? I do not think I ever saw a handsomer or nobler-looking man."

" Yes, rather good-looking," replied his lordship.

" If he be as rich as he is handsome," interposed Lady Gwendoline, " and is as open to marriage, as if he were a Christian, what an awfully great sensation he will make in Society this season. What do you think, Miss De Vere?"

"I don't know what to think," replied Laura, with a repetition of the word *think*, which pleased me, as betokening a sense of humour, "except that I think that ladies think a great deal too much of marriage now-a-days, and think that there is nothing else worth thinking about."

"Very good," said Lord Stoney-Stratford, "though I myself think it's very natural for girls to think on the subject that they think interests them most, especially if they cannot otherwise think at all."

"Hear my thought," said I, preparing to depart with Laura, "which is, that Mr. Rameses will prove a very hard man to please. It is not mere beauty that will captivate him, nor wit, nor accomplishments, nor wealth, and that he is just as likely, if he should ever fall in love at all, to fall in love for a mere caprice of his fancy, whether the caprice be fixed upon a duchess or a shop-girl."

"Shop-girl!" said Lady Gwendoline. "What a dreadful, horrid idea!"

"But he's a gentleman," said Lady Ethel, "and would never dream of such a thing?"

Mr. Bangles, Q.C., expressed his opinion that there would be at least a thousand aspirants during the season for the honour of becoming Mrs. Rameses, if the tales of his wealth were true ; even if he had only a quarter of the money which Rumour, always disposed to exaggerate, attributed to the handsome and mysterious personage.

And we separated with the conviction strong in my mind that, if there were to be a bride at all, Bangles, Q.C., had not greatly over-estimated the possible number of the candidates for the possession of the heart, the name, the diamonds and the ducats of Mr. Rameses.

CHAPTER VIII.

PHYSICAL SLAVERY AND SPIRITUAL FREEDOM.

I saw and heard nothing of Mr. Rameses for a fortnight after the dinner at Lord Stoney-Stratford's. He then wrote to say how wearied he was with London life, and how refreshing it would be to his mind and body if he could run down to the Rookery, to the groves and meadows—far away from the hot pavements, the stifling streets, and the still more stifling balls of the fashionable season. He could not find a soul in London, he said, with whom he could interchange ideas. There was talk and gossip, and babble all around, but no conversation except on inane subjects which he did not care to discuss. He wanted to bathe himself in sunshine and pure air, to tread the green grass under the blue sky, and to enjoy a little sympathy, which he thought he could enjoy in my study. Of course I pressed him to come, and he came. My mother did not seem particularly well pleased at the idea of the "Pagan" —so she called him—being installed in my house. She had a misgiving that his presence in the Rookery would turn out, somehow or other, to be unlucky. My sister and family had taken their departure, but Sir Henry de Glastonbury and his wife still remained, and it was not necessary to consult them as to what visitors I should receive. Laura was somewhat awed at the mystery that enveloped the life and character of the handsome Oriental; and rather hinted than openly expressed her opinion, that it might be well if she were allowed to remain in the background during his visit, and that she should not be called upon to entertain him in any way.

It was clear that she had not found in him a twin soul to her own, and that there was no mutual sympathy between her and him. I told her that Mr. Rameses desired privacy—that he would pass the greater part of his time in my library, among my books, my Chaldean slabs, and my Egyptian papyri; that very probably his hours would be absorbed in study, or in the unrolling of the mummy, so long waiting for its opportunity, in which grand ceremonial only he and myself would be permitted to share—and that the kindest course the ladies of my household could pursue towards him, would be to let him alone, and not to expect him to associate with them, either at morning, noon or evening repasts, unless he expressed a decided wish to do so, which I did not think he would.

It was upon these conditions that he returned to and was accepted at the Rookery. He left strict orders at his London hotel, that no letters, papers, or telegrams should be forwarded to him ; obedience to which orders he took the precaution of securing, by refusing to give his address.

" Do you not· think," enquired my daughter, " that Mr. Rameses broods too much over some secret sorrow, and that it would be wiser on his part not to shut himself up as a recluse, but to mix freely in society, which he seems so well qualified to adorn ? "

" Perhaps you are right, my dear, but he is the best judge of his own mind, his own heart, his own likes and dislikes, his own pleasures, and his own work. And as for solitude, it has no terrors for a full mind. The full mind enjoys it—more especially when it is in its power to break loose into society, when solitude grows irksome."

Mr. Rameses looked fagged and weary when he arrived, and sat him down in the seat under the branching full-boled beech tree that stands opposite my study window—the glory of the woodlands, and worth travelling a hundred miles to admire. Mr. Rameses fully appreciated its beauty and magnificence, and wished that it could speak to men—as it no doubt could speak (so he thought) to its fellow trees— and that it might communicate to our unlearned ears, that have but seventy or eighty summers to live, the knowledge it had acquired of nature, though not perhaps of men and women, in the seven times seventy annual growths of its rings.

"Forgive me!" he said, "Mr. De Vere, if I come before you weary—life-weary, world-weary—weary of myself, and of all the miserable surroundings of this purgatory which we call the Earth."

"What is there to forgive?" said I. "Weariness is the result of over exertion. Night is the complement of Day; Up is the consequent of Down; East is the twin sister of the West, North of South, and Sleep of Over-exertion. You as a philosopher understand that there is no such thing as a straight line, except the straight line of eternity. Here on the earth everything revolves, and we revolve of necessity. We go up, and then we go down. *Que voulez vous?* If you are weary, you have earned the privilege of rest.

"Oh, yes, my philosophical friend. Let me stretch myself on the grass. My weariness is not the weariness of the bones, the flesh, the blood, but the weariness of the soul. To-day the animal within me—or, more properly speaking, without me—seems a drag upon my spirit. The spirit is dissatisfied with itself, and with its physical husk, the body. I ask myself why I should be condemned to button and to unbutton? Why I should be under the necessity of rising up and lying down? Why I should, like a galley slave, be condemned to dress and undress, to eat and drink, to sleep and wake, or perform any of the petty, miserable, degrading functions of animal life, which I share with the beasts? And, worse than all, why I should always be compelled to walk in one dull round of labour for life, like a donkey at a draw-well, or be doomed, like Sysiphus, to roll a stone up a steep hill and see it continually rolling down again to mock me? Life is not freedom. Even at its best it is nothing but a slavery to food and drink, to the elements, and to the law of gravitation."

"No doubt," I replied, "but it is a slavery that is very tolerable."

"Very intolerable," he said, "though, if it were not for

the needs of the body, it might in other worlds be delightful."

" But have you ever imagined the kind of world in which you would desire to live, if you cared to live at all ? "

" Many a time and oft I have dreamed of such a world, and thought that possibly, after suffering so much in this, I might be purified through deep sorrow and affliction, and become worthy to inhabit it. Shall I describe my idea of it ? '

" By all means."

" My *beau ideal* is non-existence, the Nirvana of the Buddhists, and absorption into the spirit of the Divinity of the Universe, which I believe is the ultimate end of all separate life. Meanwhile, there may be, and probably is, an intermediate state of comparative happiness—destined for the good, the just, and the wise—in which the body shall cease to be an encumbrance to and a tyrant over its superior, the soul. May there not be in one at least of the innumerable planets and suns that gem the Infinitude, a real home for immortal beings, purified, exalted, sublimated, in which life shall be really life, without the seeds of physical death in it, and in which that miserable abortion Time shall be unknown ? Time ! What is Time ? The mere twirling of a little ball round a greater one, in which the circumgyrations are measured by units instead of by myriads! In this great central sun or planet of which I dream, may there not be spiritual life without physical death? May not man, or the superior being who shall take his place in creation, be independent of the vulgar necessity of eating and drinking, and of killing his fellow-creature—an ox or sheep—to feed upon it? May not the atmosphere in that blessed planet be full of nutrition, and may not an inhalation of its glorious air be sufficient to feed the noble beings on sustenance no grosser than that which the beautiful trees and flowers of this poor world draw from the sky and the moisture?"

"I grant the possibility," said I, "and would like to believe in it."

"And then," said Mr. Rameses, "if there were no necessity for food in that divine world, there would be no necessity for clothing. The inhabitants would have no occasion to rob the sheep or the bear for their fleece or their skins, to protect themselves against the elements, or to despoil the poor silk-worms of their webs to make finery for their women. There is no impurity in Nature, Mr. De

Vere. It is clothes that suggest impurity, and the nude Divinity is diviner than a Divinity who is draped."

"A delightful picture," said I; "but would there not be a dark side to it, if these careless, happy, beautiful beings had nothing to do? If they had no wants, might they not subside into stagnation, and be no better in their unblissful state of so-called happiness than if they were maggots in a cheese, or even senseless stones? Happy are the stones, if happiness is the absence of care and effort, and thoughts of to-morrow!"

"But," said Mr. Rameses, "it does not enter into my dream, which may be a reflex of undiscovered reality, to consider that in my beautiful planet the inhabitants should be idle. Their speech should be music better than Beethoven's; their occupation should be to acquire knowledge superior to Plato's and Aristotle's; their pastime should be love—etherealised and perfected, holy and ever holy. In our poor imperfect organisation the soul has but five outlets from the poor, restricted, cabined, cribbed, confined and wretched body—outlets which we call the five senses, though they are but three—seeing, hearing, and feeling—for touching and smelling, which help to make up the five, are but varieties of feeling. But in *my* planet or central sun, I love to think that the senses may be numberless, and that instead of three or five, the spiritualised intelligence, embodied as I would have it embodied, might have fifty—five hundred —five thousand—five million doors of sense, through which it might find its way into the infinitude ! Why not ? "

"Yes, indeed—why not ? I think your dream is philosophic, and should rejoice to dream with you. As you say —why not ? "

"And your suggestion," remarked Mr. Rameses, half rising from the green sward on which he had thrown himself, and supporting himself on his elbow as he spoke, " that my people, the people of my planet, would be miserable because they had nothing to do, falls baseless. Nothing to do? When they would have infinite knowledge to explore, and find infinite joy in acquiring it. When they would have infinite love to occupy them—in default of the infinite knowledge—that could never pall upon them, but from which they might seek to emancipate themselves or a change of delight. Where could be the room for misery, for discontent, or even for the weariness that oppresses me now as I speak ? "

"I grant you all this ! But *cui bono ?* "

" *Cui bono ?* " replied Mr. Rameses with a groan. " Yes, *cui bono ?*—the old eternal question about everything, even to the Great Creator himself, as some presumptuous idiots have dared to do. It is, however, the *cui bono* of this world that perplexes me. Were it a question of the other world that exists in my imagination as a possibility of the future, I should be happy to sleep on for ever in the faith of my dream, a dream far better than any reality I have ever known in the course of more than one existence."

I did not say, but I thought, that Mr. Rameses had dreamed so often the very same dream of a previous existence, that it had become a reality to him, that he firmly believed in it, and that he had wrought out in his own mind—by the same process of invention that a great romancist writes a romance and creates characters that to him are living men and women, even while he knows that they are but the progeny of his fancy—and that he could if he would narrate to me all the feelings, emotions and experiences of a previous life that he never lived, with a coherence, a possibility, a sequence, and a general truth to nature and to possible fact, that would stand the test of

6 *

critical examination as strongly as if they had been history. And as for History, what is *History ?* Who can tell whether it is truth or falsehood, and if a mixture of both, what is the per-centage of the lie to the truth in the whole adulterated mixture ? Thinking thus, I expressed no surprise at the hallucations, for such I deemed them, of Mr. Rameses, but resolved to study him with psychological curiosity, without any more references to or reliance upon the truth of his facts—or supposed facts—than would be necessary for the study of Shakspeare, or any other great writer who has built up fictions more enduring, and possibly more real, than any of the records of history—often blurred, and always more or less shadowy. Who for instance was King Arthur ? What do we he know about him ? Nothing ! Who were Hamlet and Sir John Falstaff, and Bailie Nichol Jarvie ? And what do we know about them ? Everything ! They are our intimate friends, better known to us than Smith, or Brown, or Jones, or any other people that we meet at the club. On this principle I resolved to study Mr. Rameses, to take him for granted, and ask no questions of myself as to his *bona fides,* his sanity or his insanity.

CHAPTER IX.

LURULA.

THE twin soul, concerning which Mr. Rameses so often expatiated with great and often sorrowful enthusiasm, did not appear to me to be so extravagant an idea as the ladies of my household considered it. My mother said nothing, but looked as if she could have said much, if the matter had been worth her while to discuss; while Lady De Glastonbury, more aggressive, was not only inclined to laugh, but *did* laugh in scorn. But scorn is a poor thing at best, and Lady De Glastonbury's scorn did not—as the Americans say—amount to much. I, being favourably inclined to study the idiosyncrasies of Mr. Rameses, as those of a commanding intellect, possibly out of the circle, thought that, whatever else there might be in the notion, there was no particular novelty in it.

What, for instance, is Love between a young man and a young woman, in the blossoming spring-time of their existence, but the search for the twin soul? The idea of the twin body is of the flesh, fleshly, but that of the twin soul appeals to the most occult and sacred sympathies of that great outlying world of nature, which infinitely transcends the experiences of merely physical life, a life which we share with the flowers, and the trees, and the oysters. What, for instance, does it signify, and in what does it minister to our higher existence, even in this world, if a youth and a maiden love the same fruit, the same wine, the same amusement, the same physical joy? But if they are inspired to distinct emotion by the same strain of heavenly music, if they feel unspeakable but communicable delight in their hearts, in the beauty and the glory of the same landscape, of mountain, of wood and wild, and ocean—if they are inspired by the same noble thoughts, expressed in the noblest language; if the con-templation of the starry heavens on a clear night, when the overarching sphere is begemmed with rolling worlds, each, perhaps, more full of life, joy, and beauty and intelligence, than our own little grain of sand that lies sweltering on the shore of infinite immensity—if these delights fill them with thoughts that no language can express, that glances from eye to eye, that kindles from touch to touch, that travels from smile to smile—is this unity and duality, and perfect sympathy of soul with soul a thing to be laughed at ? Let the dreadful Mrs. Grundys who block up all the highways and byways of society, with their prejudices, their meannesses, their mountainous ignorance, their titanic commonness, and their all pervading spite and conceit, laugh if they will. Their dreary mirth is as natural to them as the bray is to the donkey, and the cackle to the goose. But I believe with Mr. Rameses in the ineffable bliss of the twin soul, though I must confess that the possibility of finding it stretches itself far away into the nebular infinitudes of Belief. But the twin soul is within the bounds of possibility, even in this world ; and if it can be found in marriage—then is marriage that brings the twins together, the nearest approach to Heaven which exists on this side of the celestial gates.

The day after the return of Mr. Rameses to the Rookery, the London carrier brought him a trunk, the arrival of which he seemed to expect with some anxiety. He informed me that it contained two sets of rich oriental apparel of ancient style and fashion, as used in the days of Belshazzar, one for a man and one for a woman, which he had caused to be made at a fashionable milliner's. He had much difficulty, he said, in making the milliner and her people understand what he wanted them to produce for him; but as soon as they were satisfied that he had money enough—even though the price they might demand were five hundred per cent. in excess of what it ought to be—the difficulties in the execution of his orders (which they greatly exaggerated) vanished, and his orders were executed with the utmost deference to his wishes and caprices, as the more caprices he had the more they were prepared to be delighted with him and to charge accordingly. I forbore to ask him what purpose these exceedingly rich dresses were intended to serve, but he informed me in the evening as we sat alone in the library in desultory chat, that he had found, soon after he had first made my acquaintance, that we two, under his immediate supervision, should, at the first convenient opportunity, proceed to the unrolling and unswaddling of one or more of my mummies.

"I should like," said he, "to proceed with this work, and if perchance we succeeded in revivifying the embalmed body and summoning a soul back to take possession of it, a physical garment would be necessary, if the returning mortal should walk the earth again and be seen of mortal eyes. But there must be no interlopers, no spies, no eaves-droppers, and no incredulous fools lurking and prying and sneaking about, to interrupt—even by the opening of a door, or a sound out of season—the solemn work in which we shall be engaged. To bring a long-departed soul from the far infinitude in which it has been circling like a comet for two or three thousand years, and link it again to the physical body which once belonged to it, is a task which no incredulous person, with profanity in his thought or a sneer on his lips or in his eyes, can be permitted to witness. Pos-sibly nothing may come of the experiment. The mummy which we shall unrol may be an utterly dead mummy, or the mummy of a fool unworthy of revival, and as incapable of second growth as an ear of mildewed corn, or its little soul undeveloped in its mortal life may have long since passed into the body of a mouse, a bird, a fish, or a mos-quito, or even of a more vulgar insect, and even in that of an animalcule, floating about invisible in a drop of water, but living for all that, and eaten or being eaten as the great economy of nature may command."

"But do you really think that within the compass of

the extremest possibility—the dried-up mummy of the dead body that has been reposing, if not rotting, in the bosom of the earth that knows it no longer, can ever again receive the quickenings of the immortal spirit ? "

" You have heard, no doubt, of the grains of corn buried with a mummy, and replanted after three thousand years, when the mummy was exposed to the light of day, that sprouted and grew and reproduced themselves. And if a grain of corn, why not the human frame ? "

" But the grains of corn never actually died, their vitality only slept and hybernated, but the mummy from which they were taken was indubitably dead."

" I cannot say that I have any particular hopes of this particular mummy ; but, believing as I do that intelligent and invisible souls pervade the atmosphere, and are ready to enter into any body that they may find vacant, whether the body of a child newly born, that requires a soul that it may prove that it is alive, or the shell, not utterly defunct, of a once sentient being such as the mummies provide, I cannot deny that a mummy may be made to live again."

" I do not altogether deny, but I very greatly doubt.

Who or what is man, that his dead form should be capable of re-animation, any more than that of the rose or the lily, which bloomed in their appointed season, quite as beautifully, perhaps more beautifully than he? If men can claim this privilege of revival, why not his dog, or even his cabbage? All these live their time, and what more than our time can be expected for us, even though we may call ourselves lords of the creation and superior, while we live, to all other living creatures?"

"Aye," said Mr. Rameses mournfully, "but the rose and lily, cabbage and dog, expect no immortality."

"How do you know? Did you ever talk to a rose, lily, a cabbage, or a dog, on this great subject?"

"I grant you no. It is a pity that we cannot interchange ideas with animals and plants. If we could talk to them, and they to us, it is probable, and indeed certain, that we should learn of them many things that it would be important that we should know. Why are these barriers fixed between the different varieties of this poor miserable mortal life? I believe in perfect faith that I could learn something from a butterfly if the butterfly and I could understand each other."

"A very portentous 'if,'" said I, "and if from a butter-fly, why not from a worm or a bee?"

"Yes," replied Mr. Rameses, "and though these barriers exist between the living, do they exist between the dead—the revivable dead—the immortal spirits that once possessed bodies, and that may possess them yet again? When we talk of a dead body, and say it is the body of a great man departed, a thing left behind by its former possessor, do we not admit by the very phrase that the great man still lives, and was once the owner of the thrown-off covering of flesh and blood and bones, for which he had no further use, and that he still lives to provide himself, temporarily, and perhaps permanently, with another, and possibly a better, garment of blood and bones than that which he, still living, leaves to us, to do as we please with—to bury, to burn, to dissect? When I speak of MY body—does not the '*me*' and the '*my*' affirm that 'I' differ from my 'body,' and that the thing is not *me*, but once belonged to *me*?"

"Indubitably," I replied. "You speak to *me*, through *me*, to my body and my physical organs of sight, feeling and intelligence, which, however, are not me, but things that belong to me temporarily, and to use as long as they are servicable to *me.*"

"Just so, and if the spirit that formerly inhabited the dried-up mummy—which we shall find with its case in yonder corner—should come back, saying, 'I am here, and this body belongs to *me* now, as it did three thousand years ago,' shall we not believe what the spirit says?"

"Yes, if it says anything, and if we do not cheat ourselves, by thinking or believing that the speech is extraneous to our own imagination, and not the phantom of our own disordered thoughts."

"Ay, there's the rub. We scarcely know what is within us, what is without us, what is far beyond us, so bewildered are we in the mist of our senses—which so lead us, and so mislead us, that we scarcely know the difference between the clear, bright sunlight that shines above, and the fog that enswathes us round about."

While he thus discoursed Mr. Rameses, carelessly and but half consciously, directed his notice to the smaller sarcophagus of the two that I possessed. Looking now at them through a powerful magnifying glass, such as merchants employ when they would test the fibre of textile fabrics, he examined the lines of the ornamentation on the lid. Suddenly concentrating his attention on a portion of the design which I had often admired for its beautiful but complicated workmanship, he submitted it to a careful scrutiny through his glass. After a study of a few minutes, he pronounced it to be an inscription bearing the name, age, and date of death of the person enshrined within. " In the fifth year of the reign of Thoth, died Lurulà, priestess of Isis, in her twentieth summer." " Such," he said, turning to me, " is the record upon this sarcophagus. Is it not suggestive of youth and beauty prematurely removed from the earth? And Lurulà! What a noble name—the light, or treasure of the day! Three thousand years and more have the mortal remains of Lurulà lain within this husk and shell. Were it mine to aid in and accomplish their revival, to re-endow them with the soul which they have temporarily lost, what a glorious task and privilege it would be! What a delight it would be to behold Lurulà herself—to converse with her, bringing back, as she might do, the knowledge of which she died possessed. We might compare it—at least, you and I might—with that of our time, which we vain gloriously, and with superabundance of self-conceit, believe to be far in advance of all the wisdom of the days of Thoth, and all the other Pharaohs, and of the priests, prophets and philosophers of ages thousands of years anterior to the Pharaohs, who have left neither record nor name behind them. Pharaoh is not a name, but a title, as you know. This will be a great, a solemn, a holy experiment, my friend, to discover, or if not to discover, to attract the wandering and eternal soul of Lurulà, far up, perhaps, among the stars—circling blindly among the comets, may be—and attract it down to this dim spot, the earth—this small corner of the earth, where you and I live and breathe at this moment—and lead it back again into her long-neglected home."

"But," said I, with a sense of Euclid and the multiplication table strong upon me, with a faith or a superstition in the superiority of matter—at least in this material world —to spirit, where spirit is either not understood at all, or misunderstood, by people who think that they comprehend, and don't * * * I had a whole cannonade of "buts" to discharge upon him, of which these two were the preludes, when he courteously interrupted me by deprecating the expression of any doubt, and requesting that there should be no further discussion during the experiment, even though the experiment should seem odd in its inception, and strange and even absurd in its progress, and though it might extend over a much longer time than either he or I anticipated.   All this was agreed upon, and, though utterly incredulous as to the re-animation of the mummy, I was content to be a student of the incomprehensible, and not to vex by vain questions the mind of the experimenter. Nothing further upon the subject was said that evening.

CHAPTER X.

THE BUTLER AND THE GARDENER.

NEXT morning, as soon as I appeared in the breakfast-room—being, as usual, the first to descend to the morning meal—preparatory to a turn in the garden and the inhalation of the fresh air of early day, which I consider a medicine, the venerable-looking Mr. Binns, the butler, who had been up an hour before me, requested an audience. Of course it was granted, on the supposition that it referred to my wine-cellar. Binns met me on the gravel path, and with a solemn air, after a few awkward apologies and stammerings by way of introduction to the weighty matters that were to follow, gave me notice to quit.

"Oh, very well," said I, quite unconcerned, for I had known him for a long time to be dishonest, though I had no very ardent desire to be disembarrassed of him, lest I should get a worse in his place, "but what is your grievance?"

"Oh, nothing to speak of—at least, not until lately; but

you see, sir, I am growing old, and I and my missus are going to set up a public."

"Very good. I wish you joy and prosperity. But what do you mean by saying you had no grievance to complain of *until lately ?* "

"Well, sir, I didn't wish to speak of it, but since you ask me, I must say, sir, that I am a Christian."

"Who denies it? You are, I suppose, as much of a Christian as the rest of us."

"I don't pretend to be better than my neighbours, sir, but there *are* things no Christian can stand."

"Very likely. Don't you have enough to eat and drink? Don't you have the run of the larder and the cellar ? "

"Don't mention it," said Binns apologetically. "I have nothing to complain of on that score, especially on the score of the cellar. You trust me to judge of your wine, and I judge of it, and I take care to the best of my experience that your wine merchant shall not defraud you by sending you bad wine, and charging you for it as if it were first-rate. But it is not that, sir ! It's a case of conscience, and I make bold to say of our common Christianity, sir."

"Is it possible, Binns, that there can be a question of what you call common Christianity between you and me?"

"No, sir, not between you and me, but between me and the foreign gentleman, and his valet and body servant or slave, or whatever else he may be called. Why, they are both of them heathen infidels, sir, and their goings on is shameful, and enough to bring down the fire of Sodom and Gomorrah on the Rookery."

"In what way?"

"Why, this very morning, sir, only an hour ago, I saw both of them on their knees, clasping their hands, looking towards the sun, and praying to him as if he were God Almighty. I can't stand it, sir! I'm afeerd of the consequences!"

"Well, Binns, I won't argue the question with you. The faith of Mr. Rameses is not my faith, but I can respect it all the same!"

"Respect hydolatry sir! I can't; neither can I stay in a house where such goings on is permitted, or, as I would say, winked at."

"Well, Binns, if the world is wide enough for Mr. Rameses and me, it ought to be wide enough for Mr.

7*

Rameses and you. To what and to whom he prays is no business of yours or mine! Is your mind quite made up?"

"Quite, sir. The hydolatry and praying to the sun, sir, is too much for me."

"Say no more—but if you determine for the remainder of your days to be as great an enemy of false doctrines, false pretences, and false speaking, and of all that is not fair, honest and above board, as you appear to be of idolatry and the worship of the sun, you will be a very estimable member of society."

Binns appeared to be surprised, and as if he would gladly have continued the controversy, if controversy it were; but I turned upon him so suddenly after delivering my shot at him, that he had not a chance to add a word before I was out of sight. Binns drank more of my wine than I did myself, be it understood, and was otherwise objectionable.

Sir Henry De Glastonbury was much amused. His wife inclined to sympathise with Binns, but my mother and daughter, quite irrespective of the religious question, were rather glad than otherwise to be rid of my venerable butler, whom they more than suspected to be a hypocrite, and who moreover gave himself airs of such authority in the house as were not always agreeable.

The gardener was a man of another stamp. He knew all that had happened between Mr. Binns and myself, and the cause of it, and had ideas of his own about the butler, about the sun, and about sun worship, and as in the intercourse between us, I being my own head gardener and he but my deputy, we had often exchanged ideas, he was emboldened to speak his mind about what he called the "cantankerousness" of Binns in objecting to the religion of Mr. Rameses. "What's the odds," he said, "if you be a Christian, a Jew, a Chinaman, or a Parsee, such I think is the name of Mr. Rameses' religion, if you are true and good and scorn to tell a lie, or rob, and swindle, or murder, and love God and your fellow creatures? I think a Christian is as good as a Jew, perhaps better, and a Jew as good as a Christian. There are some Jews as is better than some Christians as I knows of, and have heard tell of."

"No doubt," I said, "that charity is the foundation of all religion, that of man to man, and of man to God. Charity, though not everything, goes a great way towards the sum total of our adoration."

"And where's the harm," said the gardener, wiping his forehead, " of thinking that the sun is God's right hand, as it were? Excuse me if I be too bold, I don't mean any offence, but when I see as sure as Spring comes round every year what the sun does (and what could be done without him?), I think that the Parsees, as you call them, are not so very far wrong after all in believing him to be, I will not say God Almighty Himself, oh no ! but God Almighty's prime minister, so to speak, in this world—that is as regards trees and flowers, and vegetables and fruits, and for the matter of that as regards men and women. Could we live at all—I am not a larned man, sir, as you know, but I make bold to ask could we live at all, any more than the trees and the yarbs (herbs the poor fellow meant)—without sunshine ? I say no, sir !"

I do not wish to be too palpable and direct in attributing motives (especially bad and mean motives) to anyone, but I cannot help remembering, apropos of this conversation, that Mr. Rameses, greatly admiring the perfection to which Mr. Pipps had brought some varieties of roses in my garden, had *tipped* him with two sovereigns. This may not account, or it may, for the good opinion entertained by my gardener of the sun worship of Mr. Rameses. I don't think Mr. Rameses ever " tipped " Mr. Binns. He did not admire or drink the liquors which it was the province of Mr. Binns to take care of and dispense, a fact which may account for his forgetfulness or disinclination, whichever it might have been, to purchase the good opinion of my very Christian butler.

I told Mr. Rameses of the Binns incident. His first impulse was to absolve Binns from blame, and to depart, rather than there should be any difficulty, or a divergency of interest between me and a good old servant, whom it might be impossible adequately to replace. But I resolutely opposed the idea, and would not listen to any of the remonstrances which Mr. Rameses thought himself obliged to make to me upon the subject. At last he yielded on the point, with the less reluctance, after I let him know —as I did very emphatically—that I did not think the loss of Binns to be any loss at all, but rather a gain to my wine cellar, and to my comfort, in having no longer to be civil to a domestic who abused my confidence, and made a hypocritical pretence of piety as a cloak to his dishonesty.

CHAPTER XI.

MODERN CIVILISATION.

I LET Mr. Binns understand that, after his unnecessary assumption and ill-mannered display of superior theological wisdom, and his thereby implied attempt to dictate to me what religious company I should keep in my own house, his presence had ceased to be agreeable to me, and that the sooner he packed up his effects, and took his departure, the better I should be pleased. The strong impression made upon the mind of Mr. Rameses by the incident seemed to be one of intense astonishment at the audacity of a person in the position of a butler in presuming to discharge himself from service for such a cause, which was about as absurd, he thought, as if one of my horses had discharged himself from the duty of drawing my carriage because of the objectionable morning prayers of a gentleman whom I chose to receive in my house as a guest and a friend. He brooded on the subject with as much wrath as a Carolinian or Virginian cotton planter, half a century ago, might have displayed if one of his field negroes had given him notice of his intention to leave his servitude and establish himself in a shop in New York or Cincinnati, on account of a difference of opinion between himself and his master.

In the afternoon of that day, in a saunter through my garden and grounds, Mr. Rameses dwelt pertinaciously on the subject of the unsatisfactory relations between masters and servants, employers and employed, which was characteristic of modern civilisation. At last we rested for awhile on the rustic bench under the shadow of my beautiful beech tree, while he opened out the whole subject, and sought my opinion upon it.

"Modern civilisation," he said, "appears to me to be founded on a wrong system, on a base and unworthy philosophy, the love of self, and the presumed right of every man to do as he pleases, in virtue of his manhood, irrespective of his knowledge or his wisdom. In fact, the curse of the present day is too much liberty, too much license of individual action, and too little action, or power of action, for the conscience of the aggregate state as distinguished from the divergent consciences of the small men who form big nations ;—the growth, in fact, of the great democratic idea that all men are wise, that the voice of the people is truly the voice of God, and that the majority of men—bad, silly, ignorant, self-willed, and wrong-headed as they may be, and often are—have the right, as they unluckily have the power when they are united in political parties, to impose their will upon and to govern the wise minority."

"I think with you," I replied, "that the tendency of modern civilisation is to establish an unwholesome despotism of the ignorant many over the enlightened few; of the hewers of wood and the drawers of water over the thinkers and the planners; of the mere distributors over the producers and constructors; of the body of Society over its mind; and of what may be called, of the leaves and branches of the great tree, over its sustaining roots and vivifying sap."

"Precisely so," said Mr. Rameses. "The civilisation which prevails in the West in the nineteenth century after the birth of Jesus of Nazareth, though said to surpass, does not even equal, that which existed in the East three thousand years before that event. If we come to think of it rationally, freedom in the mouths of the multitude is like a word screeched by a parrot, used without thought or understanding. In point of fact and of reason, there is no such thing as absolute freedom—of thought, of will, or of action.

"Everything, animate or inanimate, in the Universe, is subject to fixed, inexorable laws, which must be obeyed under heavy penalties from which there is no escape.

"The stars and planets, and all the countless orbs of space, are not free to wander from their orbits, or to disobey any one of the laws that made them and uphold them in their appointed places.

"In the little earth on which men live and die, no man is free to do as he pleases. The physical, the intellectual, and the moral laws surround him, control him, coerce him, and compel him to obedience.

"When men agree to live together, liberty is only liberty by reason of its restriction. Freedom cannot be maintained unless a certain portion of it be renounced for the guarantee of the remainder.

"The liberty of any nation is of necessity a compromise, a chain of compromises, by which the few for the sake of the many, or all for the sake of each, are restricted from flying out of the circle.

"Restricted freedom produces law and order; unrestricted freedom, were it possible to exist, would immediately produce anarchy and the destruction of Society.

"There are several varieties of freedom which in modern times are much discussed, ardently advocated, and to a certain extent, established. These are—free government, free land, free labour, free sexualism, free discussion, free thought, free trade. There is no freedom in any of these except in name. They are only reputed to be free by a careless fashion of speech, and an equally careless acceptance of words without a clearly defined meaning. There are but two out of the seven I have enumerated, namely, free discussion and free thought, which in a certain degree may be thought to be actually existent and accurately defined; but even these two are but partially free, within certain very narrow limits.

"In this disquisition of mine—precise and clear, and imbued with the wisdom derived from ancient intuition rather than from modern experience," continued Mr. Rameses, "I have laid bare the secret of the civilisation of past ages, such as men knew it in the days when Nineveh, Babylon, Memphis, Thebes and Palmyra were the centres of knowledge, power and glory; before such transient shows of civilisation as Greece and Rome arose in the world to supersede the government and the ideas of heroes and giants by those of cowards and pigmies."

"Your opinions, Mr. Rameses," replied I, "are based upon the supposed advantages of despotism over those of a free government."

" Doubtless," he replied, "the Divine Government of the world and of the universe is a despotism—uncontrolled and uncontrollable by the meddlesomeness of foolish men, who think themselves wiser than God. God's laws are always despotic, and may not and cannot be broken or impeded save at the cost and to the punishment of those who break and would thwart them. Can a man jump from the top of a high precipice, without paying the penalty decreed by the law of gravitation? Can he offer his body to the consuming fire without being burned? Can he abolish the immutable laws of geometry, and make a straight line crooked, while still preserving its straightness? Can he call upon Annihilation to annihilate anything? Can he destroy even the smallest atom that God has created or reduce any something, however small, mean, and imperceptible, into nothing ? He cannot. Despotic law, invariable, invincible law prevents him. We all say that in the Almighty Ruler of the universe there can be no change or shadow of turning, and concentrate the great idea in the phrase ' I am that I am, and ever must and shall be.' There is no absolute Liberty in the Universe, and there cannot be. Were there Liberty the whole microcosm might shiver itself into fragments, to await the action of the mighty hand that should reconstruct them again into order and into beauty, and to the divine action of authority and law. 'Order,' as your poet says ' is Heaven's first law, and includes every other.'"

"You once hinted to me that you might be tempted to attempt to win a seat in the British Parliament. I suspect you would have no shadow of a chance, with your notions, of acquiring the favour of one voter out of ten thousand."

"If I did give such a hint," replied Mr. Rameses, "I must have been suffering from a temporary fit of madness. To be the nominee of a caucus ! Faugh ! To be the so-called free slave of a thousand fools, would be unspeakable slavery, intolerable degradation—from which my soul would revolt, if my body played my soul so false as to submit me to it ! In public affairs, were I ever so foolish as to mix myself up with them, I would be '*aut Cæsar aut nihil*,'—*aut* more than Cæsar, *aut* less than nothing."

Mr. Rameses and I never spoke of politics again. The subject was odious to him, and more or less alien to my tastes.

CHAPTER XII.

THE PALIMPSESTS.

MR. RAMESES, as we sat together under the shadow of my venerable tree, and for which I have a respect that is of a fervency approaching to enthusiasm, both on account of its beauty and longevity, unexpectedly enquired of me if I had ever thought on the subject of palimpsests and on the possible multiplicity of them that yet remain to be deciphered and explained?"

"No doubt," I answered, " there have been many that are now hopelessly lost. Ancient parchments are rare, and carelessly treated by ignorant and indifferent people, who do not know that under the modern writing traced upon them may lie concealed many treasures of knowledge of the bygone time. The monks in their religious zeal for the multiplication of the Gospel narratives, and in the scarcity of materials for books that existed before the invention of printing, were accustomed to write over with the blackest possible ink, the faintly legible but invaluable manuscripts which were dimmed and nearly obliterated by time, neglect, and hard usage."

"And it has never struck you," he asked, "that the human brain partakes of the nature of a palimpsest? That the facts, the thoughts, and the experience of bygone days recorded upon it may remain indelible, though written over and temporarily effaced by the newer impressions it receives in the progress of time?"

"Possibly," I replied, "if we did but know of, and could take advantage of, the old lamps, temporarily extinguished by the superior brilliancy cast by the new ones."

"And may not these palimpsests of the immortal mind be as truly indelible as the palimpsests that are to be perceptibly and carefully traced on the perishable papyrus or parchments of our remote ancestors, recoverable from the misty Past if circumstances, affinities, sympathies and the eternal harmonies and connections of all Time and Nature assist in the patient process? The human brain is like a sensitive musical instrument—silent, inert, irresponsive, and niggardly of its hidden wealth, until it is touched by the skilful fingers of some gifted musician, or by the breath of the passing wind, that draws from the strings of the quiescent Eolian harp the wild weird melodies that slumber within it—melodies that may be near akin to the eternal harmony of the spheres."

"A fair subject for poetical fancy," I replied; "but one that will find few adherents, except, perhaps, among the Theosophists and Rosicrucians, or among the electricians—who have given us the telephone, and enabled us partially to become independent of Time and Space and set their trammels at defiance."

"Time," ejaculated Mr. Rameses, with a slightly contemptuous curl of his upper lip, "is an old impostor. We have conquered him in the future by electricity, and can girdle the earth in forty seconds, as Shakespeare's 'Ariel' asserted she could do, and made him actually of imperceptible account. We can also conquer him in the past, though to less useful purposes; and we do so, to a great extent, when we look at the stars in the constellations of Orion and Andromeda—which we see, not as they now are, or may be to-day, but as they existed myriads of years ago, when their light first began to reach our melancholy orb, Even the Polar star, that shines so brilliantly in the midnight sky of our Northern latitudes, may have ceased to exist ten, or a hundred thousand years ago, though it is still visible to our sight. To the eye of the immortal mind, the past is present, just as the present will become the past before we have ceased looking at it. I often bewilder and please myself by diving down into the mysteries of the by-gone ages, and living such portions of them once again, as suits my waking—or possibly my dreaming—fancy. Only last night I wandered in imagination on the Plains of Shinar, and learned from Nimrod the secret motive of his great undertaking in raising the tower of Babel."

"And I dare say you thought," I remarked, "that he was no impious madman, as the world has supposed, but a great, natural philosopher, and far in advance of his age and people, and of the natural science of his time?"

"He is supposed," continued Mr. Rameses, "to have lived about five,thousand years ago, but the palimpsest which I fancy I have been able to decipher on the brain tablets of my memory, cleared of the mythological errors which have been inscribed on the original manuscript, shows me the real intention of his mind in building his mighty tower. It was not designed for any profane, or blasphemous, but for a highly scientific, purpose—in the midst of a barren plain,

8 *

on which no moisture fell, but which if fertilised by rain, as he thought it might be, would grow corn and fruit to feed the clamorous multitude, that increased too fast for the means of subsistence which the country afforded. He knew that a constant accumulation of heat on high places draws down to earth the superabundant water that floats in the clouds ; and his object in building his tower—not to reach Heaven itself, as the ignorant multitude supposed, but to overtop the clouds—would, if a fire of sufficient dimensions were kept perpetually burning on the summit, infallibly draw to the thirsty earth the beneficent life-producing rain, and cause the barren wilderness to smile with flowers and fruit, and the brown and barren ground to become green with succulent grass."

"The supposition is ingenious, and not by any means unphilosophical or unscientific," I replied, as Mr. Rameses warmed in the exposition of his imaginative theory, which I endeavoured to support by the citation of such modern facts in its corroboration as had fallen under my cognisance. "Do we not know," I asked, "from the experience of such great cities as London, Manchester, and Glasgow; that in consequence, it is to be fairly assumed, of the multitude of tall chimneys that are continually pouring heat—which is electricity—into the atmosphere above them, a greater quantity of rain falls than in the adjacent thinly inhabited and fireless districts? After any tremendous battle has been fought, accompanied by the explosion of enormous quantities of gunpowder, rain is made to fall within a few hours, or even during the progress of the battle. Are we not also informed, on the indisputable authority of living witnesses, that a similar result invariably follows a great naval engagement upon the ocean?

"Such facts as these, in reference to the action of heat upon the atmosphere, had been studied by the ancient fathers of the world more thoroughly perhaps than by the money-worshippers of this age, and shallow-minded children who expect philosophers to think for them, and never think for themselves, and if they do think, for the most part think wrongly. But they were wholly unknown to, and un-suspected by, the Jews, to whose tradition the story of Nimrod and his tower are traceable, whose vulgar and un-worthy idea of the great Creator and Governor of the Universe was that he was fashioned like themselves, subject to the same infirmities and passions as they were, and that h and his fellow-gods, of whom he was represented as continually jealous, were really afraid that Nimrod would succeed in building his tower, to reach the no longer safe altitude which was the supreme God's own appointed dwelling-place. Poor fools! not to have reflected that Nimrod might, if he had lived so long, have continued to build until the crack of doom, ere he had reached the upper strata of our atmosphere; and that if material and patience endured, a hundred years' work would not have carried the crazy structure to the height of Chimborazo, or even of little Etna or Vesuvius!

"And then the folly of imagining that such a hopeless expedient as to confound their language, and render their speech unintelligible·to each other, was the only means to render impossible, or, at least, difficult, the consummation of their impossible project!"

"The confusion of tongues, so called," replied Mr. Rameses, "was indeed a confusion of voices, of which the modern world has every-day experience whenever men congregate and dispute. I believe that it consisted on the Plain of Shinar of nothing more wonderful than the angry vociferations of an excited multitude of discontented labourers who had struck or resolved to strike work, either to compel their employer to increase their wages—a boon or a demand which Nimrod would not grant, or with which he was unable to comply. Or the mighty hubbub may have been produced by the utter want of faith on the part of the clamorous crowd in the alleged utility of the unremunerative undertaking, on which the tyranny of Nimrod lavished their wealth and wore out their bones. This is my reading of one of the palimpsests that Time has spared.

" But it is not the only one that has been buried alive in my memory, or covered by the dust of ages—not lost or wholly obliterated, but only encumbered, dimmed, and choked up by the ruins under which it lay hidden. My second palimpsest is a Babylonic one, and dates back for nearly six hundred years before the commencement of the Christian era, when the great Belzhazzar reigned and held his court.

"In the beautiful city in which I seem to remember that I served as a priest in the Temple of the Sun, I have an idea that I was present at the great festival which the King was engaged in celebrating, even when the conquering Medes and Persians were thundering at his gates. Belzhazzar, the meaning of whose name is 'the servant of God,' assembled more than a thousand guests, most of them of the priestly order, to eat, drink, and be merry. Amongst them was the Hebrew Daniel, whom he had caused to be named Bel-Te-Shazzar, not the servant of the god Bel or Baal but a servant in the House of Baal—a distinction that marked his inferior rank in the hierarchy to which he had been admitted as a sign of especial favour. In the midst of the rejoicing—as the ancient Book records—a spectral hand appeared, luminous amid the surrounding gloom, and wrote upon the wall in letters of blazing light, in full view of the King on his lofty seat, with his loveliest queens and concubines around him, the mystic words, MENE, MENE, TEKEL, UPHARSIN ! The language was understood by the initiated priests alone, but was utterly incomprehensible to the Chaldean monarch, and to the greater portion of the joyous assembly. The inscription was accomplished through the agency of electricity, with all the secrets of which the priests of antiquity were as familiar as the scientific enquirers of the present day—perhaps even more so. The young, pleasure-loving, and handsome King, as history and tradition record, was sorely puzzled and alarmed, and Daniel, having acquired the highest reputation in Babylon as a soothsayer, magician and prophet, was called upon—as he doubtless expected to be—to explain the mysterious words—purposely hidden in a language unknown to the King and to the crowd, and only intelligible to the illuminati and the initiated. They are freely and somewhat loosely translated in the English Bible, ' MENE; God hath *numbered* thy kingdom and finished it. TEKEL; Thou art *weighed* in the balances and found wanting. PERES; Thy kingdom is *divided* and given to the Medes and Persians.' It is evident from the translation that the prophet amplified single words into sentences, and that these words were intended by their framers to say much in little, as was customary with the priests and priestesses who presided ove the so-called oracles of the gods. Tekel, or Tekle, should more correctly have been rendered *Teiche uile!* ' escape all of you'; and *Upharsin,* which appears in some of the versions to have been handed down to us as *Peres*, might more properly read, *gu farsuin,* or 'widely'; *teiche uile— gu farsuin,* 'escape all, and scatter yourselves widely !' The Persians were at the gates in overwhelming numbers, and this advice was the best that the priests could have tendered under the circumstances. The unhappy Bel-shazzar rushed out and perished in the endeavour to escape, with great numbers of his subjects. 'In that night,' says the Book of Daniel, 'was Belshazzar the King of the Chaldeans slain.' What became of the Jewish prophet, and whether he was arrayed by the conquerors in the scarlet robes and golden chain that had been promised him, I never enquired, but mingled with the flying crowd that took refuge in the lovely hanging gardens of the noblest city that ever perhaps was built. This also is a palimpsest."

CHAPTER XIII.

THE DREAM OF AMENOPHRA.

"I HAVE reason to believe," said Mr. Rameses, "that of the two souls which once animated the two embalmed bodies which have been encased during so many centuries as mummies within the two sarcophagi which you have the good fortune to possess, one was doomed at the time of its departure from this earthly sphere to revisit its former dwelling-place, and in a new and possibly superior form to undergo a probation to fit it for a higher and purer life in the stars. The other, who had been less blameful and more pure in the conduct of its mortal life, was destined to ascend to its reward in the Heaven of Heavens—the Holy of Holies—to enjoy beatitude for ever. The name of the first soul, as I read it among the hieroglyphs on the lid of the sarcophagus, was Lurulà, as I have already made known to you, a priestess in the temple of Isis, and of the other, Amenophra, the daughter of Memphra, a Pharaoh who reigned over Egypt in the days of the Patriarch

Joseph, the fortunate Hebrew whom he made the steward of his household and the prime minister of his kingdom. Memphra, sometimes called Rameses, was one of the reputed builders of the pyramid of Cheops, that yet stands on the banks of the Nile to preach its mighty homilies on the vanity of human wishes and the immeasurable presumption and arrogance of mankind."

The soul of the priestess of Isis, according to the belief of Mr. Rameses, yet haunted the earth, ready to be re-embodied in female form, to play a part in the great comedy of human life, while that of the beautiful Amenophra floated in the region of the stars, and was still able to hold converse from the Empyrean with the souls of those whom it had left behind in this lower world. Strong in this faith, as a reverent worshipper of the great world spirit of which Amenophra, as well as himself, was an emanation, he believed that she was able to communicate to him a portion of the secrets of the universe.

For the purpose of studying the two sarcophagi, Mr. Rameses shut himself up in my study on the night of the full moon, that streamed brilliantly on my books and my busts, and on the pictures on the wall. By his earnest desire I left him to his solitude—and his dreams on this occasion—to read by the full radiance of the unclouded orb which sailed placidly over the clear blue sky, a written Arabian manuscript, familiar to him, though unintelligible to me, who was unable to decipher a single one of the beautifully-flowing characters in which it was written, although I knew several words of Arabic picked up from books in the Roman character. He required, he said, to study a few directions for the careful unrolling of one of the two mummies, which he expected to find either in the Arabic MS. or the hieroglyphs so copiously pourtrayed upon the lids of the sarcophagi.

For this purpose he remained during the whole night in my solitary library, alone with the books, the mummies, his thoughts and his dreams; and when I entered the room in the early dawn of the following morning, I found him asleep on the comfortable arm-chair in which I had left him. On my entrance he greeted me with a placid and happy smile, and beckened me with a wave of his delicate white hand to sit down beside him. "I have had a dream," said he, "'which was not all a dream,' a revelation of mysteries that are not all quite such mysteries as are supposed, and have held converse with a soul, in the soul's language, and been told of things which, in the words of your great poet, Milton, were 'never heard in tale or song from old or modern bard, in hall or bower,—unattainable by the gross and carnal multitude, but partially attainable by the earnest truth-seekers, who know and feel, as Shakespeare says, that there are more things in Heaven and Earth, than are dreamt of in our philosophy. Shall I tell you my dream? It was as vivid to my mind as a reality; more real, perhaps, than many of the vulgar palpabilities with which we are surrounded from our cradles to our graves, and which are the unsubstantial shadows of unimagined realities."

"Go on! Dream or no dream, I hope to be edified by it."

"By the aid of charms and spells, and incantations—all of the simplest kind—which I derived from the lore of the Magi and the Rosicrucians, and the prophets and seers of a more earnest and a more reverential time than the present, all based upon the magnetic influence that pervades all nature, I summoned the spirit of Amenophra from the upper spheres, where it circulates among the countless happy and eternal emanations of the

Great Father of the Universe. The star Ione, which Amenophra inhabits, is one of the orbs which revolve around the sun of our system, and seems to be the magnificent planet with its four attendant moons which we call Jupiter, compared with which our little Earth is in bulk no larger than a pebble on the beach when measured against an island. In that mighty world, the abode of myriads of happy spirits that once endured the bondage of flesh, the great curse that afflicts humanity is unknown—the cruel necessity that compels us to fight against the penalty of daily death, and to procreate creatures as miserable as ourselves, by eating, drinking and digesting. The wholesome atmosphere supplies all the nutriment the ethereal body requires for continuous life and happiness. The inhabitants of Jupiter inhale it in every breath and exhale it pure and perfect as they receive it. Pain and diseases are unknown to them. They do not thrust poisons into their delicate frames, or contaminate their life-currents by rebellious liquors. They are, moreover, endowed with a greater number of senses than we poor earth grovellers; and are not confined as we are to five doors and windows of sense, as outlets or inlets to the wonders that surround them.

Men's five senses are resolvable into the one sense of feeling. The eye feels the light, and we call that operation seeing; the ear feels the sound, and we call that result hearing; the nose and the palate feel, and we smell and taste accordingly. Our flesh feels the contact with matter, and we call touch a sense. The senses of the inhabitants of Jupiter are not so restricted, but are as innumerable as their thoughts, and every one of them administers to their ease, their pleasure, or their delight. Their eyes are both microscopic and telescopic; they can pry into and examine the great and the small, the near and the remote, and can appreciate the magnificence of littleness and measure exactly the pettiness of immensity. To their fine ears all sounds are musical; the flow of waters is a perpetual melody; the quivering of the leaves on the forest trees is a chorus of gladness; the voice of the cataract and the roar of the ocean are like holy psalms or resounding anthems, singing praises to the great God of the stars and of the happy creatures that inhabit them.

"All that live and move on this beautiful planet are their fellow-creatures, with whom they can hold pleasant converse. They can hear the flowers talk and make love to each other.

The birds of the air tell their secrets to them. All created things of a nature lower than their own, confide in them and love them.

"Their fairy bodies are so light, so flexible, and so strong, and are endowed with such capability of rapid movement, that locomotion is as easy as thinking, and they can float on the waters and in the air with as much facility as sound can travel through space ; the exercise of their volition being all·that they require to surpass the swiftness of the eagle in its flight. They need no dull mechanical aid of wind or tide, or of wings, to bear them wherever they list to go. The four fair moons that shed a mild radiance on their balmy nights, are not forbidden to their visits. Distance to them is in reality as non-existent as on the earth and ocean, when the electric current virtually abolishes it by speeding over the telegraphic wires to carry the thoughts, the needs, and the desires of the long-estranged nations of the earth to each other.

"And not the least of the many blessings which the inhabitants of Jupiter enjoy, in a world where eating, drinking, and garments are unknown and unnecessary, is that there is no grinding, grovelling selfish trade, no systematic robbery, no warfare of the strong against the weak for the means of sustaining life; no false weights and measures, no adulteration and poisoning of commodities; no lawyers, no doctors, no malefactors, no sick people; no rich, no poor. All the inhabitants are happy, and industriously intent upon acquiring the knowledge which opens its illimitable stores before them and satisfies and fills their lives with perpetually recurring joys, each joy greater than the joy which preceded it, and all conducing to adoration of the great Creator of the Universe, at the threshold of whose bright abode they stand, with permission to enter into the boundless Paradise of which their temporary home is but the vestibule.

"Amenophra unfolded all these mysteries to me—every one of them within her own glad experience since she left this earth four thousand years ago."

"And do Amenophra and the inhabitants of Jupiter never sleep?" I interrupted Mr. Rameses by asking. "And if they sleep, when, where, and how does the divine forgetfulness fall upon them?"

"They sleep at will, untroubled by a dream, on the leaves of the great water-lilies that grow in the clear waters of the lakes and rivers, or they float quiescently upon the fleecy clouds that adorn the blue sky, and prevent the monotonous beauty of the expanse from palling upon their sight."

"Your description of the happiness of Amenophra tempts me to long for the death of the earthly body, and inspires my mortality with a passionate longing to put on immortality. I think the ideas with which she has inspired you of the abodes of the just are infinitely more worthy of contemplation than the Mahomedan Heaven resplendent with lovely houris and teeming with physical delights, or than the Christian Heaven with its golden pavements, its gates of pearl, and its superabundance of priceless jewellery, such as our common-place preachers in synagogues and conventicles amuse themselves by imagining. But all possible descriptions of the possibilities of Heaven fall short in beauty of the description of the great Scottish preacher, Dr. Chalmers, who affirmed that Heaven was not a place, but a state of mind. Herein lay wisdom, philosophy, poetry, and imagination, and nothing can surpass it in truth and beauty."

"Granted," said Mr. Rameses, "to its fullest extent. It

9*

is the state of mind which, according to the spirit of Ameno-phra, exists in Jupiter.   Heaven is truly a state of mind, as Hell must be, whether the Heaven or Hell exists in Jupiter or on this earth."

"Very poor and mean are man's notions of Heaven," continued Mr. Rameses, "but quite consistent in their littleness with the narrow intelligence vouchsafed to him, and with the vulgar physical delights which are all he can appreciate in a vulgarly physical world, where eating and drinking are the acme of his enjoyments, and the penalties entailed upon eating and drinking are the acme of his sufferings.   Truly considered this earth is but a purgatory, a reformatory, a prison for the peccant soul to be furnished with a body—though, happily, not to be enslaved to it for ever."

CHAPTER XIV.

SOME days after the conversation recorded in the last chapter, the subject of the priestess of Isis, Lurulà—dearer to his fancy than her sister Amenophra—was renewed between Mr. Rameses and myself. "Is it really your belief," I enquired of him, as we sat alone in my study, surrounded by sarcophagi, by rolls of papyrus, and by ancient slabs inscribed and indented by hierographs, in cuneiform characters, "that it is the hard fate of the priestess of Isis—your well-beloved Lurulà—to endure again the bonds from which Death released her?   And in her second state is the memory of her first to remain fresh in her immortal mind? And can she, and will she, if you succeed in establishing relations with her, recall the circumstances in which she played a part in the childhood of the world?"

Mr. Rameses replied sorrowfully :

"I dream of her as my twin-soul, and I know that my dream is true, from the infallible indications of electric sympathy which possess me when I think of her, and strive to trace her earthly progress since our fates were separated. I cannot tell if we shall ever meet on this side of eternity. All is drear and dark, and the palimpsests of my memory are not susceptible of complete restoration in this world. She may have passed through many gradations of existence, since she ministered in the Temple of Isis—gradations of being, doing, suffering, remembering and forgetting, loving and hating—if such a divine soul as hers is capable of hating—or of living and dying. But I have had a dream of her, as I have had of Amenophra—a dream of her sorrow, almost of her despair; a dream of her unfulfilled desire and of her weary wandering through the wilderness of this lower earth—in the as yet fruitless quest of her twin soul.

"Last night the wind howled dismally through the trees of the Rookery, though you, perhaps in sound sleep, did not hear it. But I heard it as I lay dolefully awake. It piped amid the dark branches of the yew and the cypress, and amid the fresh green boughs and leaves of the oaks, the beeches, the birches, the lindens, and the elms; and my vagrant imagination distinguished a rhythm, a coronach, a rune, a wail, as of the priestess of Isis lamenting her doubt and her desolation which seemed to say in the words of a poem that has long lingered in my memory—

' Merciful Mother Isis, take me back into thy bosom.
   Take me back ! oh, take me back !   I have wandered from thee long,
   I have strayed in doubt and sorrow through a wilderness of darkness,
   Ever searching for the right, ever lapsing to the wrong.
   Take me back ! oh, take me back ! repentant and heart humbled,
   To the high embattled fortress of thy love that cannot fail ;
   For I'm weary, very weary, and I long to rest my spirit
   In the shadow of the glory of thy never lifted veil.'

"This chant—for such it seemed to me—of a despairing spirit, was faintly familiar to me—as if I had heard it in a previous state of existence, and vaguely and but half remembered it.   It passed and re-passed through my brain in the long night watches, in spite of my will, and of my strong determination to banish it from my mind.

"I slept fitfully, and, in my dreams, seemed to remember that in the first flush of my early and passionate manhood I was a priest in the temple of Isis, in the city of Thebes.   The pyramids, at that early period, were reputed to be of venerable antiquity.   Their purpose, their utility, and their origin were surmised, but not known. I was devoted to the priesthood from my boyhood, and became an exponent, as far as I was able, of the inner

mysteries, and of the awful words inscribed upon the por-
tico of the temple—'I am all that is, all that ever was, and
all that ever shall be; no mortal has ever lifted my veil.'
The countless worshippers of the goddess believed in her
with unquestioning faith, and considered her to be the
arbitress of human destiny; the bride and sister of the
Sun, who was the fountain of life, knowledge, and happiness, the ruler of the seasons, the source of all possible
fertility in man and nature; without whose aid the propagation of all plants, and animals, and every form of life, in the
heavens and the earth, and in the waters, was impossible;
who regulated the motions of the planets, and maintained
the stability of the Universe. As my contemporaries
believed, I believed also. Of Isis, and the Sun, her lord
paramount, I was the minister and the slave. So entirely were
my mind, my body, and my soul, to be devoted to the service of the Temple that all human affection—if I indulged
it even by a thought, a word, or a look—was considered a
crime against the all-powerful hierarchy of which I was a
member—an act of treason against the Majesty of Heaven.
The punishment decreed against such weakness of the
flesh, was not alone the solemn and ignominious degrada-

tion from the ranks of the priesthood, which was invariably inflicted upon it, but the loss of life itself, as far as life could be lost in the eternal universe, by the laws of which death was impossible. But, alas! for me! The Divine electricity that throbs in uncontrollable pulsations through all space and time, and animates every created thing, and compels the union of body, as well as of soul, in all that live and breathe, and more particularly in man and woman, made me feel that I was a man, and drew my soul to a radiant woman of unspeakable beauty, who was a priestess at the shrine. I knew it to be written in the records of eternity that I should love her as man has always loved woman, and, priest as I was, I yielded to the pleasant destiny that seemed opening out before me.

"But the young priestess received my silent homage as unconsciously as the sun received the homage of the lotus that grew on the banks of the Nile, and opened its leaves to the kindly beam of the noonday sun, and responded not to it.

"But for having dared to aspire to her, and broken in my heart the vows of celibacy which I had taken on entering the Temple, I was sentenced to death by the High Priest of Isis. I suffered the penalty—with perfect resignation to the will of Destiny—without pain, quietly, as if sinking into sleep, dreaming a pleasant dream, and cherishing the consoling hope that, as Death was but the door that opened into eternity, I should meet again the beautiful object of my earthly adoration, and wander with her through the gardens of Paradise, no more to be separated from her, but living in perfect unison with her for ever and ever. Such was my dream. Was it not a palimpsest and a revelation ? "

" I think not," replied I ; " only the result of a disordered nervous system, and of too much brooding over one all-engrossing subject that had too long held possession of you. A long walk, followed by a warm bath, will restore the equilibrium of your mind. Try these remedies."

Mr. Rameses, while retaining his idea, said he would act upon my advice. He did so, and the subject was not again renewed between us ; though I cannot doubt but that he still clung to the truth of his thought, and nursed his spirit in it.

CHAPTER XV.

In the spring of 188—, the following paragraph appeared in what are called the "Society papers," that administer to the high and low bred gossip-mongers of London, the pabulum on which they love to regale themselves :

"We learn, on the best authority, that the celebrated Parsee or Hindoo millionaire, Mr. Rameses, has purchased, at an almost fabulous price, one of the most superb mansions in South Kensington, which he has just completed furnishing in a style of princely magnificence. He intends, during the approaching season, to give a series of entertainments, including dinners, garden parties, balls, concerts, *al fresco* theatricals, and masquerades, to which only the *élite* of the very *élite* will be invited. He has secured the services of a distinguished *cordon bleu*—one of the most famous gastronomes in Europe—formerly in the service of a Royal personage, and has engaged to pay him the highest salary ever yet paid to a cook, and a stylish brougham for his exclusive use. The income of this Asiatic potentate is said to amount to at least £150,000 per annum, so that the sinews of war will not be wanting to keep up the splendour of his *avatar* in London.'

Whether the writer—a fair and aristocratic penny-a-liner moving in aristocratic circles—knew the meaning of the imposing word *avatar*, it is not necessary to enquire.

Another journal, of the same class, announced during the

following week, also on the "best authority," that there was no foundation for the current rumour that—

"An Indian millionaire, at whom countless fair widows and still fairer spinsters are setting their caps, presumably in vain, is about to put an · end to all these silly reports, by joining his hand in holy matrimony to that of the lovely and accomplished daughter of a noble house—the fairest of the three remaining unmarried daughters out of a family of seven, all happily —and, indeed, splendidly mated."

It needed far less knowledge of the great world of London —its doings, its jealousies, and its intrigues—than that possessed by Lady Stoney-Stratford, to convince that clever personage that the paragraph referred to one of her daughters—though to which of them she was unable to say. But the announcement set her ladyship thinking of a thing that was not, but that might possibly be, at no distant date, if she played her cards properly. The prize to be striven for was great and splendid, and fairly accessible to what the great revolutionist, Danton, called, "*de l'audace, de l'audace, toujours de l'audace !*" Some envious people call this valuable quality, "skilful management"; though mere skilfulness sometimes fails, when audacity is not audacious enough. Lady Stoney-Stratford was not deficient in either quality, as the great world of London, especially that small portion of it called "Society," well knew; and although it sneered at her more or less persistently for the reputation she had thereby acquired, admired her all the same, and recognised her as a notable match-maker, and a very superior woman.

Lady Stoney-Stratford's opinion of the possible bride-groom that might, if all went well, be secured for Maud, Ethel, or Gwendoline Pierrepoint—she hoped it might be for Gwendoline—was somewhat dubious of his sanity. All the world admitted that he had strange notions about a "twin soul," and the felicity of the life to come; but after all, she thought, such notions were harmless, and as for sanity, what was sanity? She could not tell exactly. Even her husband was accused by the malevolent world of not being perfectly sane, because he borrowed money at ten, twelve, and sometimes fifteen or twenty per cent. per annum to invest it in acres that did not yield a third or a quarter of the amount, and—whatever truth there might be in the charge—no man living, or woman either, was perfectly sane on all points. Had not the French poet, Boileau, of whose writings she was a professed admirer, said that all men were mad, and only differed from one another in the degree? And had not a still greater poet, Dryden, intimated that it was rather an honour than otherwise to be mad, inasmuch as great wit was nearly allied to madness, and only divided from it by thin partitions? The "fad" of Mr. Rameses, as she called it, about the "twin soul," was a romantic and rather praiseworthy fancy, and she sincerely hoped the estimable millionaire might find the anticipated twin in the bosom of one of the Pierrepoint family, to share his thoughts, his love, his sorrows, and his millions.

It was one of the greatest consolations of Lady Stoney-Stratford's life that all her daughters were "good" girls—that is to say, they never set their fancies, their caprices, their whims, or their predilections, in opposition to those of their mother when marriage, or the possibilities of marriage, were concerned. In fact, they were all as docile as French girls before the event of marriage, and during the progress of the negotiations that led to it; and understood as well as any French mademoiselle the conditions of the "absolute monarchy of the mother," to which they had to submit in their apprenticeship to the trade of life, a temporary maternal despotism that was to be followed by the pleasures and unrestricted liberty of a democratic republic, as soon as they became " one and indivisible " with a legal proprietor.

The Countess, it must be said, was not altogether easy in her mind with regard to the manageableness of Lady Gwendoline, who was more skittish than any of her sisters— a skittishness resulting from her too great familiarity with horses, and the life, language, and manners of the stable— though the mother was reconciled to the comparative way-wardness of her daughter by the knowledge of her over-powering love of money, and of the horses, the carriages, the grooms, the coachmen, the diamonds, and the amusements, that money could purchase. Her indulgence in slang was, as her mother rightly thought, a convincing proof of her high appreciation of money, and of all the coarser joys it could bring her; so that, all things considered, she relied upon Lady Gwendoline's docility, patience, and skill, when she was told to angle for Mr. Rameses in the stream of Society, where there are very few fish of his dimensions to be caught.

Whatever Mr. Rameses did, it was his pleasure to do thoroughly; and in resolving to play the part of a leader of fashion in London society, during, at least, one season, it was his intention to eclipse in taste and splendour, if it were possible to do so, all other leaders of fashion, from the Prince of Wales downwards to the most successful railway contractor, or owner of silver mines in Nevada, or diamond fields in South Africa. He had the will, the means, and the recklessness to do as his inclination dictated, and though he anticipated no enjoyment—except that of having his own way, which neither he nor any other human being was ever known to revolt against—from the heavy labours he knew that he was assuming, he hoped, at least, to have the advantage of taking a lesson in life's hard school, and of making the acquaintance of some of his school-fellows, and of learning much that was good, or at least useful, for him to know, both in the playground and the study.

In his desperate plunge into the vortex, to make a figure in London society, and to spend his money like a prince, he was determined to have his money's worth in experience of all that Society could offer him—in splendour, in excitement, and in what is called "sensation"—so that when the brief period of his cometary life expired, he might be remembered as long as Society could remember anything, and be looked upon as a wonder for one day more than the customary nine which the fates allow to all abnormal celebrities. In the ideal world of London Society, Mr. Rameses had a vague kind of feeling that amid its eddies the "twin soul," of which he could not prevent himself from dreaming, might appear when least expected, not necessarily upon the surface of the great stream, or on its banks, or even in its depths, nor on the highways or by-ways of the much trodden thoroughfares of the mighty city. He did not trouble himself to think whether the "twin soul" would appear in the shape of a young, artless, and radiant member of the aristocracy, or of a daughter of the middle classes,

> " Poor, perchance,
> But rich in native elegance,"

or of a village maiden, gathering primroses in the fields to adorn the bosoms of the true believers in the faith according to St. Beaconsfield, or even of a lower grade—a flower girl standing at a street crossing, offering to the passers-by her innocent wares—as innocent as their wares, to all outward seeming. To him, amid the clouds and vapours in which he lived, moved, and had his being—all gifts of rank and fortune, all endowments of worldly goods, all personal graces and accomplishments, were alike unconsidered and inconsiderable, if not infinitesimal, compared with the great and predominant idea which had taken possession of his dreaming fancy, that of discovering the "twin soul," if such a soul existed either on the earth, or in the planetary spheres, from which it could be summoned at his bidding.

Of such "twin souls," he maintained that the records of history, as well as the traditions of Romance, Poetry, and Mythology, were full. Was not, he asked himself, the fair Hero the twin soul of Leander? Heloise of Abelard? the Beggar-maid of King Cophetua? Laura of Petrarch? Juliet of Romeo? Ophelia of Hamlet? Cleopatra of Antony? And in a much lower scale of intellect—Nell Gywnne of Charles II.? Josephine of Napoleon Buonaparte? Madame de Maintenon of Louis Quatorze? Mrs. Fitzherbert of George IV.? and Mrs. Jordan of William IV.? And was the twin soul of Mr. Rameses non-existent? He could not think so; she might be Lurulà, or a *prima donna* in a London or Paris theatre, or even a ballet girl unknown to fame or the footlights. He might be destined to find her, or he might not; but still, though undiscoverable in Time, she might be discovered in Eternity.

The hypothesis of a twin soul, as necessary to the felicity of married life, was, according to Mr. Rameses, not an idle fancy, or a fond aspiration after the unattainable, as the thoughtless are apt to suppose, but a life based upon nature and necessity. It was his firm belief that souls emanate from the giver of all life in twins. Positive and negative electricity, light and darkness, up and down, attractive and repulsive, are twin-born, and exist from all eternity. The one is the completion and the corollary of the other, the perfect chord in the heavenly harmony, without which music would be but a clash of jarring dissonances. Who finds the twin soul and is happily united with it, finds as much of heavenly bliss as it is permitted to mortals to enjoy, and remains in perfect union with nature and his kind, and with the whole surrounding universe. In perfect alliance with the twin soul, there is no such thing as discordance of taste, temper, or aspiration. To think the same thoughts, to feel the same joys, to be affected by the same sorrows, to be moved by the same impulses and passions, or even to be stirred to exertion or melted to softness by the same breath of melody and music; or to feel the same sympathetic currents coursing through one's veins, and sparkling in one's eyes; to love what the twin soul loves, to hate

10*

what the twin soul hates, if hate be possible to the immortal spirit—this is to know what happiness really means in a world where antagonisms are the rule, and accordances are the exception. Those who find the twin soul, and are made one with it, need not dream of Paradise, for they have passed its portals, and the angels have welcomed them into the blessed domain, from whence expulsion is impossible in time or eternity.

All the members of the Pierrepoint family had full knowledge of the "fad," the "craze," the "hallucination," the "fancy" or the "crotchet" of Mr. Rameses—for by these several epithets they called it—and looked with more or less indulgence upon it, as not so very heinous an offence against the respectabilities, the *bienséances*, or the stereotyped ideas of the Nineteenth Century, as it might be ignorantly or maliciously considered. Lady Ethel, far more than Lady Gwendoline, sympathised with it, and thought it sweetly poetical, and not by any means to be ridiculed. Lady Maud was neutral—had not, in fact, thought much upon the subject—but was fully prepared to excuse the apparent eccentricity, most pardonable in a man with a hundred and fifty thousand pounds a year, who, if he married at all—which she did not think he would do—would marry for love, having no occasion to marry for money, or even for rank. Was not money, she thought, more than rank? And was Mr. Rameses not the reputed son of a *Begum*, or Queen, the Maharanee of Nirvanabad, and, therefore, if he chose to call himself a Serene, or, possibly, a Royal Highness, could he not do so?

Lady Gwendoline scoffed irreverently at the idea of his having a Begum for a mother, and, in her customary slang, with a woful attempt at wit, asserted—not wishing that her words should be taken *au serieux*—that the son of a *Begum* was, of necessity, a *Big-humbug*. Her wit, if such a strong word could be fairly applied to so feeble a vulgarism, was not to the taste of the Earl of Stoney-Stratford, who had the very highest and deepest respect for a man in the position of Mr. Rameses, one who could purchase thousands of acres without being reduced to the ignoble necessity of borrowing—at an exorbitant rate of interest—thousands of pounds sterling to pay for them, and whose acquaintance and friendship he was determined to cultivate. He flattered himself that it was from no desire to worship the great Saint Mammon, but from the conviction that it was

better to cultivate the acquaintance of the rich than of the
poor—especially if the rich were very rich, and were never
guilty of the folly, the sin, or the crime, or whichever it
might be, of hoarding up their money, and making no bene-
ficial use of it either for themselves or their neighbours.
In this respect calumny could prefer no accusation against
Mr. Rameses. His gold fell upon barren places like a refreshing shower, and his generosity was like sunshine wherever
it penetrated.

The reputation thus acquired by Mr. Rameses was dearly
bought, and became a source of constant annoyance.
Though an Asiatic and a sun-worshipper, he was expected
to contribute towards the building and endowment of
Christian churches and chapels without number, to the
outfit of Colonial bishops and a whole army of mission-
aries, to the maintenance of every London hospital and
charitable institution, to countless societies—malignant or
benignant, as the case might be—for the propagation or
abolition of everything, to associations of strong-minded
women and weak-minded men for the encouragement or
discouragement of anything of which they did not approve,
or for the support of measures to be taken in seaport or

garrison towns for the dissemination or at all events for the non-prevention of shameful contagious diseases, for the evangelisation of Thibet, Japan, and China, and for innumerable other bubblings up in the great, thick, slabby cauldron of restless and unreasonable philanthropy.

Then there were the Joint Stock Companies, of which the name was legion, or a hundred legions, of which the avowed objects were ten per cent. to the enterprising shareholders, and enormous gains to the contractors. Direct lines to Kamschatka through the snowy wastes of Siberia, or to the Indian Ocean through the heart of Central Africa ; for the exploitation of gold mines in Nova Zembla, Ultima Thule, and Spitzbergen ; for aërial communication with the North Pole ; or great national schemes for rendering the gas and water supply of every city, town, and village in the empire as free as the air breathed by the inhabitants ; and for turning all the wheels of the world's machinery by the power of the wind, the waves, and the water-currents, from mighty Niagara to the tiniest brooklet that winds its devious way through the meadows.

The very capacious waste-paper basket of Mr. Rameses, and the still more capacious fiery furnace of his great new mansion in South Kensington, received such cart-loads of letters, circulars, lists of directors, and speeches at public meetings, as would, if ground down and reduced into their original pulp in the paper-mills, have provided new material out of old for the imprint of "shilling dreadfuls," or "horrible pennyworths" of the lives of brigands, pirates, and burglars, and other pestiferous literature for growing boys, as well as broad sheets for the dissemination on the desecrated and disfigured walls of the Metropolis, of quack advertisements, and hair-restorers, and the sweet syrups of Mrs. Festina Lente, for the painless extinction of the too numerous infant progeny of the British Isles, and preventing them from adorning the twentieth century with their genius or their beauty. Mr. Rameses sometimes thought he would be compelled to engage a private secretary to answer all these letters ; but in the meanwhile came to the conclusion that a letter burned was almost as good as a letter answered, and that a fire in the grate was the best remedy for ninety-nine per cent. of the evil. So he prudently offered the greater part of his correspondence to Moloch.

The question of the private secretary was nevertheless a pressing one, and if Mr. Rameses was to play his part in the great comedy of life—as it unravelled itself to a millionaire in all its mazy complications—he could not afford, with any regard to his own dignity, to leave his letters entirely unanswered. His trouble was to find, to approve, and engage a trustworthy and gentlemanly person to fill the office, and vicariously to save him from seeing too much of the worst side of human nature in the multifarious demands that were made upon his purse by the impecuniously servile, or the really impecuniously unfortunate.

For this purpose he was advised to insert advertisements in the *Times*, the *Daily Telegraph*, and the *Standard*. He did so accordingly, offering a salary of £300 per annum to the fortunate candidate. The magnitude of the result bewildered and surprised him. The letters received in reply amounted to upwards of fifteen hundred. Among the applicants were retired officers in the army and navy, from major-generals and admirals down to simple lieutenants; from briefless barristers too numerous to count; from Oxford and Cambridge graduates; from the younger sons and brothers of peers—all entitled to write "honourable" before their names; from disappointed and returned colonists, who found, as they said, that there was no place like home;

from the penniless sons of penniless curates, who had been too uxorious in their early manhood, and had brought families into the world without the means to maintain them from men who were too proud to dig, and who looked upon manual labour, except with the pen, as a disgrace; from broken-down attorneys and attorneys' clerks; from third and fourth rate journalists; from promoters and secretaries of public companies, to whom a rise of salary from £100 to £300 was an object of ambition; and from the residuum of all the learned professions, elbowed out of the chance of gaining a subsistence in the hard scramble, tuzzle, and tumble of life. Among these were large numbers of what the Scotch call "stickit ministers," willing to preach commonplace and drowsy sermons, but finding no pulpits to preach from, and no congregations to weary with their platitudes. Mr. Rameses, on surveying the pile of letters that arrived from day to day, and from hour to hour, accompanied by still greater piles of printed testimonials, and in many instances by the photographic portraits of the candidates, dreaded that a temporary private secretary would be necessary before he could deal with the claims of the expectant permanent ones. On endeavouring to sort the letters as well as he was able, he discovered to his surprise that at least one-third of them were from ladies. Perhaps the "twin soul" might be among them! The thought distressed him for awhile, lest in rejecting her for his private secretary, as he could not choose but do—being an unmarried man with the fear more or less developed of the formidable Mrs. Grundy, autocrat of the English world, before his eyes—he should have banished from his presence the bright particular star of which he was in quest. But he took comfort in the thought that Fate was Fate—that he could not escape it, wherever or whatever it might be—and that the star of his destiny was much more likely to descend from the Empyrean, than to be found among the impecunious and multitudinous daughters of the middle classes of England.

And Destiny found him a private secretary beyond the limits of the fifteen hundred, in a totally unexpected quarter, in the person of a young gentleman privately recommended to him by his old friend and correspondent, Monsieur Palliasse, of Paris, as an art student, a philologist, the son of an English father born in Benares, and deeply imbued with all the learning of the East, untrammelled by the superstitions either of the East or the West, and a searcher after Truth, wherever the Truth might lead him, "convinced," he said, "that no one truth could possibly misfit with or contradict any other." To these qualifications, such as they were, he added, those of being young and handsome, a thorough man of business, an accomplished vocalist and instrumentalist, and without any obvious personal vices or prominent religious prejudices. His name was Melville, and after sufficient inquiry he was duly installed in the responsible post of private secretary to the great millionaire, and the confidential distributor of his charities. The fifteen hundred candidates, military, naval, legal, clerical, literary and Bohemian, living upon their scanty wits, of whom, perhaps, not above half-a-dozen had ever imagined that they had the remotest chance of the appointment, severally came to the conclusion that the world was a very hard world to live in, and that merit, industry, and high character were of little or no value in the struggle for existence. None of these people could do anything but write letters—not always grammatically—and cast accounts—not always correctly. They were all too proud to do manual work, though they were not exactly ashamed to beg, but found that mendicancy was an unprofitable and sometimes a dangerous trade. The women could read, and some of them could write—or fancied they could write novels and verses, and all of them could play the piano-forte ; but not one of them knew how to cook an egg, a potato, or a mutton chop. All the fifteen hundred aspired to rank as gentlemen or ladies, and many of them were so, although without the means to maintain their position, or the spirit to seek new homes in Canada or the Antipodes, where strong and willing hands were wanted. But Mr. Melville had the coveted place, and was not at all elated that he had secured it.

CHAPTER XVI

NEW SCENES AND NEW CHARACTERS.

EVERY sane man may be said to lead a double life in his progress through the world, and his intercourse with his fellow-creatures. Doubtless some insane men also lead double lives, and not only double, but multiple ones. The notorious burglar, Peace, Pease, or Pace, whatever was his name, who reduced burglary to a system, as deftly conducted as that of a General Provider or a wholesale linendrapery, was a burglar by night, while by day he figured as a respectable tax-paying householder, a musical adept, and a not illiberal contributor to the charities of the town or village in which he resided. Old Patch, the equally notorious forger of Bank of England notes, who flourished at the end of the last century, passed himself off to, and was accepted by, his neighbours as a quiet, but somewhat humdrum and prosy country clergyman, and sometimes as a well-to-do dealer in beeves and sheep and agricultural produce. Dr. Dodd, who was made by the law to feel in his neck the whole weight of his body, to his body's grievous detriment and collapse, was a noted divine, preaching eloquent sermons on the sinfulness of heterodoxy, and infraction of the sacred laws of property, enshrined in the cabalistic words, " meum " and " tuum." A once fashionable banker, of more recent memory, was a systematic robber of valuable documents committed to his charge, and at the same time a pillar of the Church, an eminent philanthropist and a bright exemplar to his clerks, who never cheated him of a shilling, for want of the will, and possibly of the power to do so, and the overpowering knowledge of the certain punishment with which their offence would be visited, if the vigilant banker discovered it and asked a jury of his countrymen to decide upon the crime. Many thousands of the aforesaid jurymen—bakers, grocers, pawnbrokers, wine merchants, tailors and shoemakers as the case may be—who would not hesitate to prosecute with the utmost rigour of the law any starving reprobates who broke into their shops and plundered the tills, act a double part and live a double life, and gain great advantage by adulteration of their goods, selling by false weights and measures, and foisting off upon the too confiding public their inferior for superior articles, and end their career as vestrymen, churchwardens, justices of the peace, and even in rare cases as members of the great Imperial Parliament, that rules a nobler empire than ever fell to the lot of Darius, Xerxes, Aurungzebe, Alexander, Cæsar, or Charlemagne.

Idiots alone are single-minded in this best of all possible worlds—that is if they have any minds at all—which is doubtful. Mr. Rameses, as a man of great though irregular intellect, one who was afflicted by crazes, crotchets, fads, and wayward fancies, was of necessity many-minded, but, as was written by Oliver Goldsmith of another person, "e'en his failings leaned to virtue's side." Though he was a man of impulse, he never allowed himself to ride Mazeppa-like on the back of a wild horse through the wilderness, and never lost the reins of his impulse if it threatened to run away with him. Though a hot enthusiast, he could if he pleased be a cold reasoner. He was a man of action as well as of thought, a materialist as well as a spiritualist, a wise man in most things, a foolish man in many things; one who performed the most generous acts when the fancy seized him, but who was sometimes parsimonious or what the world persisted in calling "mean"; one, in fact, who would cheerfully disburse ten thousand pounds on a caprice, and begrudge a shilling for a necessity. The idea of the "twin soul," which he expected to discover either in the highways or the byways of his life, was not an all-absorbing passion, but a calm anticipation of a possibility that might become a reality; and if the world sneered, and was respectfully doubtful, what did the sneer or the doubt signify to a man who had a hundred and fifty thousand pounds a year, and loved his hobbies the more affectionately the more the world laughed at them?

*   *   *   *   *   *

[Here the narrative of Mr. De Vere comes abruptly to a close, and is continued by another hand; a man who had less sympathy with Mr. Rameses in his peculiar notions of this world and the next, but was open to conviction on any point that did not conflict too violently with his somewhat sturdy and obstinate prejudices. The new chronicler of this veracious history was inclined, as will be seen, to be tolerant to other people's eccentricities if they did not take the shape of antagonism to the Decalogue. Unlike Mr. De Vere, he was fond of society and of a town life. The great maelstrom of London life, into which Mr. Rameses had plunged head-foremost, was to his taste, though not at all to that of Mr. De Vere. The pensive and philosophic recluse of the Rookery returned, therefore, to his books, his manuscripts, his mummies and his beloved garden, to cultivate his roses, his strawberries, and his drumhead cabbages—as dear to him as they were to the Emperor Diocletian, who much preferred the quiet cultivation of those magnificent vegetables to the unquiet cultivation of the votes and goodwill of the turbulent multitude of Rome.]

Mr. Rameses had requested of Mr. De Vere, as a particular personal favour, that the mummy of the Egyptian lady, whom he called Lurulà, and supposed to be that of a priestess of Isis, should be transported to his new house in Kensington. He promised that the most reverent care should be taken of the priceless relic, until the day of its solemn unrolling in the presence of and by the aid of the most eminent experts and practical philosophers, Egyptologists and cognoscenti in Great Britain, France, Germany and Italy, whom he intended to invite for the purpose. He also proposed to give them a magnificent dinner at the conclusion of the ceremony, to be attended by His Royal

Highness the Prince of Wales, and as many of the members of the upper and lower branches of the legislature as could possibly be induced to be present. He also proposed to organise a grand concert of Egyptian music, such a^s Nebuchadnezzar the king delighted in, and at which the instruments employed were the cornet, the flute, the harp, the sackbut, the psaltery, and the dulcimer. The cornet was, it is to be supposed, the shawm or trumpet; the sackbut the bag-pipe—which the Germans call *dudel-sack*, and the French with less propriety the *cornemuse;*—the psaltery was a stringed instrument akin to the lyre, the lute, and the harp, though doubtless of different construction. Possibly the dulcimer was no other than our familiar friend the violin. All Nebuchadnezzar's instruments were proofs of the civilisation of the people who invented them or adopted them, and included no such barbarous contri-vances as the drum, the gong, the bell, the delight of children and of all savage and of some cultivated nations to whom all noise is more or less musical.

The palace of Mr. Rameses, for such it might be deemed, was due to the taste and ostentation of a great railway potentate, a princely "navvy" and employer of navvies,

11*

who had accumulated a large fortune out of the labour of the multitude, and exhausted, or endeavoured to exhaust all the resources of ancient and modern art in the construction and luxurious decoration of his dwelling-place. His breakfast-rooms, his dining-rooms, his smoke-rooms, his bath-rooms, his billiard-rooms, his library, his picture and sculpture galleries, his boudoirs, his reception-rooms, and his bed-rooms, were the admiration of all who, as a great privilege, were admitted to visit them, and were the talk and the envy of London. `The lucky proprietor, for so the world persisted in designating him, built this magnificent abode, and lived in it but for three weeks, when Death, who, as we all know—though we never seek to profit by the knowledge—has no respect whatever for money-bags, sat down one day at the rich man's table uninvited, and maliciously smote him with apoplexy. He had summoned his butler to his awful presence, to remonstrate with him on his carelessness in sending up a bottle of Clos Vougeot which had been for twelve years less time in bottle than the Clos Vougeot which he had ordered. He had worked himself up into a state of excitement over the mistake which had made him look foolish in the eyes of his guests, to whom he had been vaunting the superior excellence of the liquor, honestly worth five guineas a bottle, as, in an outburst of innate vulgarity, he had taken care to inform them. The stroke was what the French designate as one of *apoplexie foudroyante*, or *coup de foudre*, and the poor rich man died at the table before the affrighted guests. The butler sought to bathe his temples and support his head, but the poor wretch never spoke or opened his eyes, and was removed in the arms of the butler and the footman. The awful event elicited from a fashionable physician who was present the safe observation, that it was exceedingly wrong of any one who valued his health to give way to anger at the dinner-table. This was a piece of professional advice which, if tendered to the unhappy millionaire before the catastrophe, might have prevented it altogether, and been well worth the fee that might have been paid for it to the Esculapian baronet.

Mr. Rameses bought this mansion of the executors of the deceased "navvy," after a vain attempt on their part to let it at the enormous rent demanded for it. But he refused to buy the library or the picture gallery, preferring to be surrounded by his own books and paintings, all chosen in consonance with his own refined taste in literature and art, and dear companions and friends of an otherwise lonely existence.

The mummy of Lurulà was duly installed in the library on its arrival, placed under a canopy of purple velvet, in a darkened recess lit up day and night by a Rosicrucian lamp, of antique workmanship, to which its possessor attributed the quality of perpetual electric illumination. Beside the richly embroidered couch on which the sarcophagus had been placed, stood an ancient Egyptian harp, with ten strings, such as is represented in the tomb of Rameses III., and pourtrayed in Mr. Chappell's erudite History of Music. This was an instrument on which Mr. Rameses looked with peculiar veneration, and to which he attributed an antiquity co-eval with that of the Pyramids. It was certainly a very old harp, but not so old by twenty-five or thirty centuries as its gratified possessor believed it to be. But he found so much pleasure in the thought that Rameses III., from whom he was possibly descended, might himself have drawn music from its trembling strings, that it would have been cruel to hint a doubt as to its genuineness;

and I therefore refrained from doing so, though some-times sorely tempted to air my incredulity and my superior knowledge.

Mr. Rameses, who had taken his young secretary, Mr. Melville—half of European, half of Asiatic, birth and educa-tion—not only into his confidence, but into his friendship and affection, and seldom suffered him to be absent from his councils or his amusements—asked and obtained the per-mission of Lord Stoney-Stratford to bring him to the great dinner-party. Lord Stoney-Stratford had expressed the pleasure he would have in making the acquaintance of the young gentleman, and the matter was arranged accordingly.

A frequent guest at Lord Stoney-Stratford's table was a person whom Lord Stoney-Stratford was often blamed by the world for receiving with so much honour; an offence, however, which the censorious world was ready to pardon, when it reflected that Lord Stoney-Stratford was not a very rich man, and that the guest he favoured was blessed with an abundant fortune. The person in question was Mr. Algernon Pigram—two incongruous names, that ought never to have been linked together. Mr. Pigram made a figure in the second stratum of fashionable, or quasi-fashionable, society in London, and was sometimes invited to a few aristocratic houses in the first stratum, because he was rich and a bachelor, or, if not exactly a bachelor, a widower. Here he occasionally mixed with gentlemen and ladies in circles which might have been closed against him, had not these two accidents—wealth and single blessedness—been in his favour. He was old, ill-favoured, vulgar, dropped his aspirates where they were imperatively needed, and picked them up and used them when they were wholly unnecessary. His personal character—though not tainted with positive dishonesty—was what is more significantly than elegantly called "shady." He seemed, like Midas, to turn everything he touched into gold, and, like Midas, was known to all men in his true character, in spite of his gold, by the long, soft ears, hairy and flexible, comparable to those of Bottom, the Weaver, in Shakespeare's inimitable play, which Fate had condemned him to wear. He had played many parts in his life, and succeeded, more or less, in them all ; but his crowning piece of audacity, accompanied by his customary good fortune, was the concoction of a pill, for the assurance of long life and health to all who would swallow it with the requisite amount of persevering faith. By what he considered the inspiration of genius, he named his pills the Methuselah Life pills, and by their ready sale to the credulous multitude he realised a princely income. His next venture, equally successful, was the establishment of a newspaper, in which he was not able to write a line or inspire an idea, but for the conducting of which he found no difficulty in hiring the intellect of which he himself was deficient. His next rise in the world was as Member of Parliament for the very small and corrupt borough of Swine's Holme, sometimes called Pig's Holme, or Pixham, to which he had been strangely attracted by the kinship of its name to that which he had inherited from his father, ·a highly respectable pork butcher. He was a sturdy supporter of the minister of the day, voting for all the measures of the Government whenever they happened to be right, and with more exemplary devotion always supporting them whenever they were· wrong, as they usually were. For these services he expected a baronetcy, some said a Viscountcy. But neither Baronetcy nor Viscountcy rewarded his zeal. The great Minister who had these honours in his gift looked with undisguised contempt upon all the mean-

spirited and needy supporters of his government who sought
for them, and was heard to speak of Pigram as a pig both by
name and nature. The great minister was accustomed to say
that he wished it was as easy to make gentlemen as it was
to make Baronets, Viscounts, and Dukes. " A true gentleman," said he, in that democratic groove in which his
thoughts were accustomed to run, though he was a born
patrician and proud of being one, " is rarer than a king,
and I have known kings and princes in my time who have
been veritable snobs—sows' ears, in fact, like Mr. Pigram,
and not silk purses."   But, fortunately for the peace of
mind of Mr. Pigram, if he had a mind, this whiff of minis-
terial disfavour was never blown into his nostrils, and he
was content to dream of the Baronetcy or the Viscountcy
as certain to be his some day, and to be an enhancement
of his matrimonial chances in the eyes of some fair aristocratic spinster or widow, who might condescend to share
either of those titles with him.   The spinster on whom he
had cast his eyes—not his affections, for he had none—was
Lady Gwendoline Pierrepoint.   That splendid young
woman—for splendid she was in physical beauty—though
she loved money much, for the indulgences and luxuries

it would bring her—had no favour to bestow upon any ugly, elderly man, who had nothing but money to recommend him. It must be stated, too, that her mind was preoccupied, and had no room for Pigram, when she remembered the handsome form, the noble features, the princely bearing of Mr. Rameses. If Mr. Pigram had had double the wealth of that princely gentleman, or if Mr. Rameses had had but half the wealth of Mr. Pigram, much as she loved money, she would greatly have preferred the poorer man to the richer " duffer," such was her word, and reconciled herself to the possession of fifty thousand per annum in lieu of one hundred and fifty thousand. After all, as she said to herself, money was not everything, and a pleasant face to look at, night and morning, was well worth a little sacrifice of ready cash. Besides, to be outraged daily by the reckless dropping of the aspirates, which was the great characteristic of Mr. Pigram's conversation, was intolerable, especially before company, all the females, and most of the male, members of which would have thought she had sacrificed herself for money, which might be true, but which, nevertheless, was not to be urged against her, even in the thoughts of her dearest friends, who blamed her, but who would probably have married a still greater "duffer" than Mr. Pigram, for the same advantages.

Mr. Rameses knew nothing of the high favour in which he stood with the bright Lady Gwendoline, nor did that beaming damsel care to consider too seriously the fact that Mr. Rameses was a Pagan, a sun-worshipper, and one who had no faith in the holy religion in the doctrines of which she and all her family had been nurtured. But these matters sat but lightly on the mind of the lady, and scarcely ever entered into her thoughts. And if they did at times find an entrance into her solitary meditations, she imagined that the faith of Mr. Rameses might sit as easly on his conscience as her faith did on hers. Indeed, she thought that all religions were more or less the same, if they taught people to believe in God, to be good, to avoid doing wrong to one's neighbours, or to anybody else, and that there was no difference, except in the form, between a Parsee and a Christian. Thus it will be seen that the Mammon-adoring lady took spiritual things easily, thought much of the efficacy of good works, and little of the saving influence of strong, or even of weak, faith, in obtaining entry into Paradise. But she seldom thought of Paradise at all, ex-

cept as a place reserved for such portions of good "Society"
as had money to spare, and liberally spared it for the building of churches, the civilization of savages, and the dis-
seminating of the Gospel among Jews and Heathens.
But these things did not half so much trouble Lady
Gwendoline as the extortionate bills of her dress-maker,
her presentation to Queen Victoria at the approaching
Drawing Room, and her appearance at an exceptionally
grand State Ball or Concert.

Lord Stoney-Stratford, in blissful ignorance of the state
of Mr. Pigram's mind and that of Mr. Rameses with regard
to his eldest unmarried daughter, invited both these persons
(I was going to say gentlemen, without reflecting that the
word did not apply to the concocter of the Methuselah
pill) to dine with him in company with Mr. De Vere and
myself, at his house in Stanhope Street, May Fair. It was
shortly after Mr. Rameses had taken possession of his mansion in South Kensington, and his first appearance in London
Society in the full blown lustre and renown of his millions.
In a *tête-à-tête* conversation with Lady Stoney-Stratford,
that strong-minded, but womanly woman, Mr. Rameses endeavoured to clear himself from the imputation of being a

dreamer of dreams, or an idle visionary, wandering through life in pursuit of a chimera, and losing his hold upon the realities of life, and with his hold upon it losing all interest in the great conflict of humanity. He desired to stand well in Lady Stoney-Stratford's opinion, though for what purpose it would have puzzled him to explain; while, on her part, Lady Stoney-Stratford was only too anxious for the sake of either one of her daughters—she did not care which—to encourage the most friendly relations with so powerful and wealthy a nabob as Mr. Rameses was considered to be.

"You are very eloquent, Mr. Rameses," said Lady Stoney-Stratford, "on the subject of the twin soul, but I would ask you how you know that the twin soul is in existence, and can be discovered either in time or in eternity?"

"Because," replied Mr. Rameses, "human souls proceed from the soul of the universe, which is God, in inseparable pairs, male and female, like all Nature one and indivisible —of the same essence, the same design, the same aim and object, the same in life, and in what we poor midges of a summer day call death, without the slightest knowledge of the meaning of the word which we use so commonly —instead of change, progression and enlargement."

"I grant the possibility of the twin soul," said Lady Stoney-Stratford, with a deep sigh, "in the next world, but not in this, and envy the happiness of him or her who discovers it. But this is a world of contradictions and not of resemblances, of antipathies rather than of sympathies—a gross world at the best, in which we and all of us are slaves to physical surroundings, and the ignoble necessities of the animal rather than of the spiritual life. I wish the twin soul had fallen to my lot, and that it may fall to yours, but I must own that I despair of it, either for myself, or for you, or any living creature. The happiness would be too great for mortal to bear, and I resign myself as in duty bound to the want of it. And, after all, the loss of what one never had or enjoyed cannot be very great. So you see I am a philosopher after a fashion, and do not trouble myself by sighing after the unattainable."

"But," said Mr. Rameses somewhat abruptly, for which he was rather sorry afterwards, "you could not have thought that bliss unattainable when you married Lord Stoney-Stratford, or you would not have married at all. If the twin soul is not found in the marriage state, it cannot, one would think, be found anywhere on this side of eternity."

Lady Stoney-Stratford heaved another sigh. "'Tis a painful subject, Mr. Rameses," she said, "and we will leave it if you please until, as Mr. Carlyle might have said, the 'Ineffable Eternities,'—as one too great and incomprehensible in this hard world of antipathies, self-seekings, animosities and divergencies. Possibly, however, to Lord Stoney-Stratford may belong the triumph of having found his twin soul in the person of one Mr. Pigram, the proprietor of a wonder-working pill, a man after his own heart, whose land abuts upon our own, and who is willing to dispose of it at a fairly reasonable price to his Lordship, for the honour of the thing, as he says, and not for vulgar personal advantage. I should like you to meet him, and expound to him your sublime theories."

CHAPTER XVII

THE DEER FOREST.

MR. RAMESES confided to me the fact that he greatly dis- liked to be present at ceremonious dinners, especially if the company were numerous, and that his beau ideal of a dinner- party was a *partie carrée* of four persons, who knew and understood each other's minds and idiosyncracies, and who could find something else to talk about than the weather, the fashion, the last new or old scandal, or the dreary, and too often acrimonious, polemics and politics of the hour. He consented to meet Mr. Algernon Pigram, solely to please Lord and Lady Stoney-Stratford. With Mr. De Vere he was more at home, and always looked forward with pleasure to the interchange of ideas with that gentleman, who was in all respects a man after his own heart, with whom he could converse on "Foreknowledge, Free-will, and Fate," and grope darkly, but still pleasantly, in the misty by-ways of occult philosophy, not to be traversed at dinner-tables, or in the company of ladies, but in the sacred solitudes of the study or the library, or in woodland rambles, where the mind was not occupied with the purely animal necessities of eating and drinking.

Lord Stoney-Stratford did not care for the conversation of Mr. Pigram, which was more monosyllabic than was agreeable to him as a man of the world, and savoured largely of the Scriptural "yea" and "nay," which, contrary to the Scriptural dictum, he believed to be evil, inasmuch as they prevented the flow of rational ideas, and acted as dampers upon polite and mutually pleasant interchange of thoughts.

Mr. Pigram, on this occasion, was in the highest of high spirits, and, in his abounding satisfaction with himself and fate, diffused his aspirates over the room with a prodigality and profusion that jarred upon the sensitive ears, and disgusted the refined taste, of his aristocratic friends. But he was unconscious of the offence he gave, and it was all atoned for and forgiven when he announced that on the previous day he had brought to a successful conclusion a long-pending negotiation for the lease, at a large rental, of a deer forest in the Highlands of Scotland, extending almost from sea to sea, and comprising an extent of many hundreds of thousands of acres of mountain and moorland, where grouse and red deer were alike abundant, and where man, with the sole exception of gillies and game-keepers, was a stranger, an interloper, and an encumbrance to be jealously excluded, lest his footfall in the wilderness should scare the sacred animals that Pigram kept for the sport of such good friends as Lord Stoney-Stratford. Lord Stoney-Stratford had been, in his youth, a deer-stalker, and an inveterate slayer of grouse and ptarmigan, as well as a patient and devoted angler for trout and salmon· in the Spey, the Tweed, and the Findhorn, and accepted with delight the invitation of Mr. Pigram to pass a month of slaughter on the Moors. He extended the hospitable invitation to the whole of the assembled party, promising the ladies the full monopoly of the rivers, and to the gentlemen the monopoly of the glens, the corries, and the hill-tops, that they might supply the poulterers of London and the great cities with grouse. In our day, grouse is not to be given away as of old—when a gentleman would have considered it derogatory to have acted the part of a poulterer's assistant, or to have condescended to sell the birds which he had bagged—when sport was sport, and not a trade, or a business, carried on with a view to profit.

Mr. Rameses and Mr. De Vere declined the honour of shooting the grouse and the deer of Mr. Pigram ; but the guests of the evening accepted the invitation with gladness and a profusion of thanks, that were evidently grateful to their recipient.   Mr. Rameses, contrary to his wont, commenced an argument with the compounder of the Methuselah pills and the lessee of the deer forest, on the iniquity of depopulating whole counties, once the home of brave men, to create a wilderness for the *feræ naturæ,* and outraging what he called the right of the people to live upon the soil, on which they were born, and which their fathers had cultivated.   "The owners of the English soil," said Mr. Rameses, running the risk of offending Lord Stoney-Stratford, " have no more natural right to the exclusive use of the land than they have to the exclusive enjoyment of the sunlight ; and would doubtless, if they were able to do so, divide the ocean itself into farms and allotments, and demand rent for them."

"I am a land-owner myself, in a small way," said Mr. De Vere ; "but as my ancestors bought the acres in hard cash from the then legitimate possessors, I do not consider that they wrongfully acquired it, and that I wrongfully hold it as their representative. But, nevertheless, I cannot avoid thinking that the present possessors of large landed estates, the representatives of families to whom the land was granted by the bygone kings who owned it on behalf of the people, upon consideration of the performance of certain duties, which they have failed to accomplish, have become usurpers, and are in illegal possession of the property of the State. The lands were granted to these adventurers—for such they were originally—on the tenure of military service, and on the express undertaking for themselves, their heirs, successors, and assigns, of defending the country against foreign invaders. Consequently, the great landlords of the British Isles bound themselves to maintain a force sufficient for that purpose, and to pay and equip all the military forces of the kingdom. This contract has not been fulfilled. They have shifted the burden, by Parliamentary agencies, which they themselves manœuvred and controlled, on the shoulders of the general public, and of the landless inhabitants of the towns. Thus have they escaped, during successive generations, the annual payment of many millions of money, and the whole cost of the national defence. By the system of deer forests, prevalent in the Highlands of

Scotland, the land has been deprived of the strong arms of the peasantry, who, in case of need, would have been ready and proud to defend the homesteads of which they have been dispossessed by the deer and grouse of the sportsmen."

"A very revolutionary idea," said Mr. Pigram, "the realisation of which would throw the whole country back into barbarism."

"I merely state the question," replied Mr. De Vere. "I have not the slightest intention of arguing it, especially in the presence of ladies, to whom political and social economy are necessarily distasteful."

"There would be much to be said in favour of the principle," remarked Lord Stoney-Stratford, "if we could begin afresh, at the point from which we started eight hundred years ago ; but the world is not, and cannot be, governed by obsolete principles and ideas, however originally good and unassailable."

"But true principles are never obsolete," said Mr. Rameses ; "or civilization itself would be impossible. Not that I think much of civilization, as the world now interprets it—a civilization of which the leading maxim is, each man for himself—a maxim which, to my mind, seems to be utterly subservient of Christianity. Each man for all other men, and the great God of the Universe for all humanity, even for the lowest member of it, would be the foundation of a far better religion. The land belongs to the people just the same as the sea does, and the sunlight does, and the love of God does—and not to the few who monopolize it, because they have the power to do so, while the sea, the sunlight, and the love of God are beyond the reach of monopoly."

The discussion, contrary to the intention of Mr. Rameses, would have possibly waxed warm, or branched off into innumerable unconnected and incongruous ramifications, had not Lady Stoney-Stratford, who had been watching the opportunity to withdraw, given the expected signal to her daughters, who all gracefully retired, and left the philosophers to their philosophy, such as it was. Mr. Rameses was the first to follow the ladies to the drawing-room, anxious to hear sung some of the melodies of Scotland, which acted on his mind and fancy—and perhaps on his dim remembrances of a remote past—with a weird and powerful fascination.

He had no sooner left the table than Mr. Pigram, finding

himself alone with the young secretary, Lord Stoney-Stratford, and myself, expressed a strong opinion, minus all the aspirates, which he could not help eliminating in his excitement, that Mr. Rameses was no better than a Nihilist, a Socialist, a Communist, or a Fenian, in entertaining the opinions which he did about the land, and especially about the Deer Forests, which were, in his estimation, one of the greatest proofs of the high state of civilization to which Great Britain had arrived—the indirect means, as they undoubtedly were, of clearing off the surplus population from the land where their presence was an unmitigated evil, and consigning them to the abounding acres of Manitoba, Australia, and New Zealand, where men were so urgently required. Lord Stoney-Stratford partially agreed with the plebeian plutocrat, but prudently reserved his opinions, as a member of the Upper House of Parliament, where they might, for all he knew to the contrary, be some day or other cited against him. Young Mr. Melville was anxious to take up the argument in defence of Mr. Rameses, but his youth made him reticent, and he held his peace, contenting himself meanwhile with nursing his wrath against the proprietor of the Methuselah pill.

Lord Stoney-Stratford maintained a good understanding with Mr. Pigram on the subject of the land which the latter was ready to bring into the market, and the purchase of which, on easy terms, was an object of great desire on the part of the territorial peer, whose greed for acres it was impossible to satisfy while an acre remained for sale within the radius of a day's walk from the country mansion of his ancestors.

CHAPTER XVIII.

MATRIMONIAL TRAPS.

LADY STONEY-STRATFORD, as already observed, was anxious that Mr. Rameses should espouse one of her three unmarried daughters—she was not particular which, though she would have preferred that his choice should fall upon Lady Gwendoline. Mr. Rameses was quite unaware of the hopes he had excited in the breast of the scheming mother of these three Graces, and had not been greatly attracted by the charms of either of them, least of all by those of Lady Gwendoline, who talked slang to an extent that, to his mind, was more than disagreeable. He had not the pre-eminent love of the horse which is entertained by so many rich and fashionable English men and women. He disliked especially to see a woman on horseback, and had a positive detestation, if not abhorrence, of the sight of a beautiful young woman, or of an unbeautiful old one, in the hunting-field, in pursuit of a stag, a hare, or a fox. He considered hunting to be an amusement essentially barbarous, or as an avocation only to be justified by the fact that the huntsman or huntswoman was in pursuit of natural prey, like the eagle in the air, the shark in the sea, or the lion in the desert, in search of the food that is necessary to their existence. For these reasons the charms of the fair Lady Gwendoline had no attraction for him, when he thought of her as a horsewoman—if he ever thought of her at all when he was not in her society. The softer charms of Lady Maud were more to his fancy, especially when he sat an enraptured listener as she sang the pathetic and tender melodies of Scotland, in a clear, soprano voice, which might have made her fortune in the concert-room or on the operatic stage. She had inherited her love for, and partly her proficiency in, Scottish music, from her mother—a member of one of the most powerful clans in the Scottish Highlands. She boasted of her descent from Malcolm Canmore, who was a king when the founder of the Stuart family was nothing more than the major domo, or superintendent, of the Royal household. Mr. Pigram had no ear for music, but he had a great admiration and love for horses, and was not averse from betting on their speed, or their chances, at Epsom or Newmarket, and preferred the language of Lady

Gwendoline to the more correct language spoken by her sisters and by the elders of the family. Between the money-hunting young lady and the money-possessing old man there was no antipathy on that score : and such antipathy as existed, was the result of difference of age, social position, antecedents, education and manners, and was not shared by the comparatively ancient person who was most interested.

The match between the two was proposed to her daughter by Lady Stoney-Stratford, who, though slow to convince herself of the impossibility of effecting a union between Mr. Rameses and Lady Gwendoline, on which she had fixed her heart, and on which she had reared a whole pile of calculations, was not slow to conceive the great advantage of a match between the rich—and she might imagine generous—proprietor of the Methuselah pills and her penniless daughter. Lady Gwendoline, on her part, was more reluctant, even obstinate, than her mother expected she would be, and brought a powerful force of her aristocratic prejudices to open a deadly fire against the alliance with the vulgar plebeian, whose only merit in her eyes—though a very great one—was his money. She even borrowed some shafts of resistance from the armoury of her mother, and maintained that a descendant of Malcolm Canmore— would commit the great crime of *mesalliance*, worse even that of *lèse majesté* in condescending to share the ducats of a parvenu millionaire. But the hideous idea grew less hideous to her mind the more she familiarized herself with it. To the ducats—still more plentiful—of Mr. Rameses no such objections attached, even though they were not the ducats of a Christian. Possibly, he was as much of a Christian, if judged by his conduct, as Mr. Pigram was; but then Mr. Rameses was not a suitor for her hand, and his money was not within the reach of her aspirations. And, moreover, she was fully aware that her soul was by no means the twin soul of Mr. Pigram, and that the mysterious electricity that attracts kindred spirits to each other, or that repels those which are not of kin, was in her case a repellant. Besides, how could she link her fate with a man of the name of Pigram? The name was odious to her mind, and she would not, she thought, be called Lady Gwendoline Pigram, or even Pogram, for all his wealth, were it ten times greater. Her mother was fully aware of her feelings in this respect, and did not like to consider it prejudice, though half afraid that it was no other, and would have been better pleased if the proprietor of the Methuselah pills had been simply named Brown, Green, Jones, or Smith. In fact she was fully convinced that the rose of Pigram would have smelled sweeter if it had been called Howard, Montgomery, Cavendish, or Grosvenor.

Lord Stoney-Stratford made light of the difficulty, and undertook to remove it in a confidential *tête-à-tête* conversation with the owner of the peccant patronymic. At least, he would endeavour to do so, and flattered himself that he should be able to succeed in it with a little management. He was of opinion that he could prove to the satisfaction of the plebeian Pigram that an alliance with the patrician house of Pierrepoint would be cheaply purchased by the sacrifice of the surname which he had inherited from his ancestors— always supposing that he had any ancestors, or could trace them further back than to his father.

As a prelude to the delicate negotiation, his Lordship invited Mr. Pigram to dinner at his club, in order that the matter might be amicably discussed between them. Mr. Pigram was nothing loth to enter into the question, but asserted, as a preliminary, that he was not ashamed of his name, but was, nevertheless, not so obstinately attached to it as to prefer it to any other. If the wife took the husband's name on her marriage, he, for one, did not see why the husband should not take the name of the wife, if sufficient reasons existed for the change, as, in fact, was sometimes done, and as had been done lately, and Mr. Algernon Pierrepoint was a name that would look well in the Court Directory or on a visiting card. Lord Stoney-Stratford did not see any sufficient necessity for this, and somewhat curtly dismissed the suggestion. He added that no man had any exclusive property in his surname, but might change it as often as he pleased, provided always that he did not change it for any fraudulent purpose, or to hide from his creditors, or to avoid legal process in a civil or criminal court. "I remember," said his Lordship, "hearing the law on the subject very lucidly laid down by one of the most eminent judges that ever adorned the English bench —the late Sir Nicholas Conyngham Tindal, Chief Justice of the Common Pleas. I was summoned as a witness in that Court, and examined by Mr. Serjeant Wilde, a blatant and, I must add, impudent advocate, afterwards elevated to the Lord Chancellorship, with the title of Baron Truro, and who married into the Royal Family of England in the person of Lady Augusta D'Este, the legitimate but unrecognised daughter of the Duke of Sussex, the uncle of her present Majesty. On that occasion, the Lord Chief Justice explained the whole law on the subject of surnames, declaring that all surnames were purely arbitrary, and that every man was at full liberty to assume whatever name he pleased, provided that he duly notified the fact of the change to any and every one who might be interested in it."

"Possibly," said Mr. Pigram, "if he obtained the permission of the Sovereign, and notified it through the Heralds' College, who would demand a large fee for its agency in the matter!"

"Quite a mistake," replied Lord Stoney-Stratford. "The permission of the Sovereign, though sometimes asked, is wholly unnecessary, and is only valuable as an advertisement. The Heralds' College is, of course, glad to clutch at all the fees it can get; and if fools choose to pay them, so much the worse for the fools, and so much the better for the officials of the College."

"But is no formality necessary?" enquired Mr. Pigram dubiously.

"None whatever!" said Lord Stoney-Stratford. "Nothing but an advertisement in the newspapers, or a circular addressed to all the friends and acquaintances of the Smith who wants to become Smythe, or the Brown who desires to make himself Green, or the Huggins who thinks that Fitz Hugh is a better name, and a request to them that he, for the future, be addressed by the new name to which he has taken a fancy. I knew a very handsome young gentleman of the name of Catt, who was enamoured of a lovely woman, and whom the lovely woman was more than willing to marry, except for her invincible dislike to be called Mrs. Catt. 'It would be very disagreeable,' she said, 'to be asked by my friends, after two or three years of married life, how the little *kittens* were, and if they had got the measles, or the whooping cough, or had been duly vaccinated. Upon that hint, Mr. Catt made up his mind to change his respectable—but not sufficiently respectable—patronymic, and became either Mr. Cathcart or Mr. Fitzwygram, I forget which. The lady of his love was delighted, and made Mr. Catt happy forthwith by accepting his hand and his new name at the altar."

Mr. Pigram appeared to be much impressed with the

argument, and the facts with which Lord Stoney-Stratford supported it ; but took time to consider the subject, and also to satisfy himself that Lady Gwendoline would accept his hand, if he really consented to the sacrifice demanded of him—for a sacrifice he could not help considering it.   He had, he thought, done nothing to disgrace the name of Pigram, which never, it must be said, appeared in the public notifications of the Methuselah pills, nor had he any right to cast a slur upon the name of his father—who had not been a farm-labourer as Lord Stoney-Stratford supposed, but a well-to-do tradesman in the county town where he first drew breath.   Would not the name of Pogram, he en-quired of himself, be a good substitute for that of Pigram, if he were compelled to change, and not too violent a departure from the original ?   Or, better still, if any alteration had to be made in deference to the aristocratic pride of the Pierre-points, would not Montmorency, Montgomery, Trevor, De Clifford, or Fitzgerald, be acceptable to the young lady ? After due cogitation he resolved, though reluctantly, to adopt, or rather to take violent possession of, the name of Fitzgerald, which, coupled with the title of a Baronet—which he hoped to acquire per favour of Mr. Gladstone—would look well, sound well, read well, and be entirely to the taste of the Pierrepoints.

In less than three months after Mr. Pigram had come to this momentous decision, an announcement appeared in the *Morning Post* that a marriage had been solemnized between Mr. Algernon Fitzgerald, M.P., and the beautiful Lady Gwendoline Pierrepoint, daughter of Lord and Lady Stoney-Stratford, and that the happy bride and bridegroom had gone to Fitzgerald's "place" at Pigram Abbey to pass the honeymoon.

CHAPTER XIX

ON THE FULL TIDE OF FASHION.

MR. RAMESES and his *entourage* is now launched upon the full tide of London life and the London season—a magnificent argosy, with all sails set, banners floating in the wind, a merry company on board, and crowds of enthusiastic spectators on the shore, cheering the full-freighted vessel as she proceeds on her voyage to the unknown shore of happiness—the new world which she hopes to discover. All eyes watch her. All pens record her splendour; all printing presses in a press-ridden land record her triumphs, and inform the expectant world of the speed at which she travels, and of the number of knots which she measures in an hour. But the sad captain sits in the cabin alone with his melancholy thoughts, coming from time to time on deck to confer with his chief mate, Mr. Melville, and to exchange courtesies with the numerous passengers of both sexes, gaily dressed, exultant and jubilant, who throng around, happy to have speech of him, and to sun themselves in the light of his countenance. The weather is calm and fair, a light, healthful breeze is blowing, and the sun shines brightly overhead.

Music and rejoicing follow on the way ; the spacious deck has ample room for the dance, that fair women love to organize, and that brave men love to assist in—not for the pleasures of the movement, but for the enjoyment it affords of close physical contact with the opposite sex, the unrestrained liberty of touch on the luxurious and suggestive waist of beauty, and the electric darts that shoot from her sparkling eyes into the susceptible and inflammable bosoms of adolescent and maturing manhood. The sad captain sees all, but enjoys nothing. His mind is far away in the ideal and the unattainable. He is as greedy of delight as Tantalus was of water ; but the delight is so distant from his grasp and taste, as to be only existent in his imagination, or sparkling with faint lustre in the future that may never dawn on this side of eternity.

His argosy is no sooner afloat in the full sight of the vociferous crowd, than he begins to feel the penalties of the full freight with which she is laden. Property, it has been said, has its duties as well as its rights ; but it may be said, with equal truth, that wealth has its penalties and persecutions, as well as its enjoyments. Mr. Rameses discovered the fact very speedily. His income, reported by the loud and quickly-wagging tongues of rumour to be of fabulous amount, loomed in the eyes of the philanthropic locusts who longed to eat it up, as large as the fair fields of Britain loomed in the eyes of the greedy Norman robbers who pounced down upon it in the time of William the Conqueror. First and foremost among the hungry swarms of devastating plagues that buzzed and hummed around him, anxious to dip their greedy antennæ into the honey of his stores, were the zealots who pretended a desire to Christianize all the heathen nations of the wide world, and who maintained in ease and comfort a dozen secretaries, clerks, and underlings, for every single heathen who pretended to be converted to the true faith, as taught by Jesus of Nazareth. Secondly came the enthusiastic would-be builders of new cathedrals, churches and chapels, tabernacles and conventicles, for the expounding of the faith to those who already believed, or pretended to believe, because they conformed to it. This numerous body of supplicants he endeavoured, and not wholly in vain, to reduce to silence and acquiescence

in the *status quo* of ecclesiastical accommodation for the
faithful, by offering to contribute the large sum of one hundred thousand pounds to a fund for the erection of a huge
Metropolitan Cathedral, upon the condition that it should
be devoted to the worship of the God of the Universe,
wholly irrespective of creeds and formulas, and that the
public would subscribe thrice that amount to the fund. The
offer was as safe to be unaccepted as Mr. Rameses surmised it would be, and the various devotees of the creeds to
be accommodated in the place of worship common to them
all, never contributed sixpence to the fund, the conditions
of which, when promulgated, drew down upon the head of
the " infidel " Mr. Rameses a perfect whirlwind of sneers and
maledictions. Next in number of the claimants of his bounty
were the spiteful humanitarians, whose name was legion
and who all had schemes for the improvement of the world
and for the means of livelihood to be provided for the secretaries of the various societies, whose ostensible business it
would be to bring the schemes to completion. Men, women,
dogs, horses, birds, and even insects, were the objects of the
regard of these busy searchers after something or somebody to
take care of ; and Mr. Rameses, who had a tender heart for

the whole animal creation, subscribed largely to the funds of such among the rival societies as recommended themselves either to his philanthropy, his mercy, or his judgment.

But the promoters of projects of so-called benevolence were not the only besiegers of his banking account. Benevolence may be a power in the world, but a greater power in governing the actions of mankind is the love of gain to be acquired without working for it, a love that controls the conduct of the rich quite as powerfully as it controls the conduct of the poor, a love that exists in the minds of plutocrats as well as in those of demi-semi-paupers and beggars, and that builds up joint stock companies, limited liability companies, for the digging of docks and canals at Panama, constructs railways, converts inland cities into seaports, distils sunshine out of cucumbers, brings the waters of the Atlantic into the deserts of Sahara, hoists a flag on the North Pole, converts Irish Fenians and dynamiters into gentlemen and peaceable citizens, and makes gloves out of the fine skins of paupers and criminals, that are now allowed to rot uselessly in the grave ; and would render gout and rheumatism impossible by the compulsory observance of a vegetable and farinaceous diet, and by the enactment of a law rendering the killing of sheep, oxen, and other animals for food not only a misdemeanour, but, if persisted in, a felony. All these schemes found adherents among the well-meaning people who laid siege to the ducats of Mr. Rameses, who found more than enough to occupy his whole time in instructing his secretary to refuse on his part to contribute a sixpence to any of them.

Nor were these the only persons who endeavoured to establish claims upon his liberality, not, however, with a view to his possible pecuniary advantage, but to their own. His name of Rameses suggested to many estimable·people of Scottish blood, whose ancestors had borne the honourable name of Ramsay, that the great new millionaire was of their race and lineage, a cousin of theirs at the very least, perhaps a cousin forty or fifty times removed, but still indubitably a cousin. On the principle that blood was thicker than water, these people, on the strength of their name and relationship, wrote to him requesting loans or gifts to set them up in business, to save themselves from the workhouse, the gaol, or the hospital, to enable them to emigrate, to establish a newspaper, or carry to profitable completion some marvellous invention that would revolutionise the trade, the manufactures, or the intercourse of the world. Mr. Melville, knowing the mind of his employer, did not trouble him with a fiftieth part of these and other applications, and returned to the remainder such answers as promised nothing, expressed no opinions, and dexterously precluded all further correspondence.

But while Mr. Rameses acted upon the principle that he would rather give away a thousand pounds of his own free will and bounty than he would be swindled of a single five-pound note, or even a solitary shilling, he was open as the day to melting charity, and devoted a large portion of his income to deeds of benevolence. As his almoner, Mr. Melville took all delicate pains, and spared no trouble, to investigate any claim that was made on his justice, his pity, or his generosity ; and the widow and the fatherless, and those who had none other to help them, received kindly relief and support from the Parsee millionaire, and found milk and honey where they had previously found nothing but hard black bread and bitter tears, and roses and lilies in the pathways where nothing had grown but thorns and thistles. None but Mr. Melville and himself knew the amount of his silent benefactions, and not even they knew the number of grateful prayers that night and morning ascended to Heaven for blessings upon the head of the unseen, and often unknown, reliever of their wants and sympathiser in their sorrows.

But the great beneficent giver was himself among the most unhappy of men. He was alone in the world—all alone—without a companion, without a mate, without the twin soul, to share his joys, his sorrows, his aspirations, and his wealth. There were perhaps thousands of lovely creatures—lovely in form, though possibly not altogether lovely in mind—who would have been willing to share his joys, and the wealth of which he was indubitably possessed, and not unwilling, perhaps, to share his sorrows, his hopes, and his aspirations ; but who could not share them to the divine extent which alone would have satisfied his sensitive being, for lack of the inexpressible, the celestial sympathy of soul with soul, spirit with spirit, which was necessary to the perfect harmony and roundness of his life. All the womankind of the upper galaxies of Society pitied him exceedingly, or even blamed him exceedingly, for wasting his days and his money in single blessedness, and deplored his infatuation—almost amounting to lunacy, in their estimation—in inhabiting a splendid palace, filled with every luxury of furniture, except the one piece of priceless furniture—a wife. And that that one indispensable article should be provided to grace the lordly mansion of the lonely hermit, was the sole object of the thoughts of possibly hundreds, but certainly scores of them. Possibly, too, some of these fair syrens were uncharitable enough to believe the unnatural state of isolation in which the prosperous gentleman was contented to live, or at least in which he lived, whether he was contented or not, might be due to the fact that he was too much married—that he had left a harem behind him in India—and that a surfeit of marriage had not only caused the holy institution to become distasteful to him, but had rendered him incapable of contracting the obligation in a Christian community. But these ill-natured sceptics were in the minority, though a still smaller minority among them were not indisposed to believe that a still stronger reason for the solitary state in which the lord of so large a fortune seemed to live, might be traceable to the fact that there was a Fair Rosamond in his bower—a fascinating Amy Robsart in his castle—and that King Cophetua was secretly espoused to some lovely beggar-maid, whom he was ashamed to introduce into the world of which he was so brilliant an ornament. But these rumours never reached the knowledge of poor Crœsus himself. And it was well, or they might have had the effect of inclining his thoughts towards cynicism or misanthropy, which was alien to his generous nature.

But the current of the aspirations, calculations and schemes of the fashionable world, as regarded Mr. Rameses, was deflected from its usual course into new channels scooped out by the holiday season and the near approach of the vagabond month of August, when foreign travel, the sea-shore, and the mountains and moors of Scotland tempted every one with money and leisure at command to leave home in search of health, excitement, or mere change of scenery and surroundings. Mr. Rameses had consented, though not without misgivings that he should fail to enjoy himself, to pass a month in the Highlands of Scotland, and to study life and nature in a deer forest, under the auspices, though not in the society, of Mr. Algernon Fitzgerald.

CHAPTER XX.

TO THE HIGHLANDS BOUND.

THE multitudinous passengers that sailed from the Broomie-law, Glasgow, by the favourite steamer Iona, included Mr. Algernon and Lady Gwendoline Fitzgerald—bound for the Highland deer forest ; hired at great expense by the proprietor of the Methuselah Life Pills. Among the guests whom he had especially invited to visit him, and who were passengers by the same boat, were Lord and Lady Stoney-Stratford, the Ladies Maud and Ethel Pierrepoint, Mr. De Vere, Sir Henry and Lady de Glastonbury, Mr. Rameses, and his secretary, Mr. Melville. The mansion attached to the extensive domain was large enough to accommodate all these visitors, and more if occasion had demanded, and Mr. Fitzgerald had resolved to loosen his purse-strings in honour of the great occasion, and to do his best to procure sport and recreation for the somewhat incongruous assemblage of people whom he had invited to pass the autumnal months in the hospitable wilderness. The company on board the .

steamer consisted of tourists, holiday-makers and sportsmen, with a large percentage among them of Glasgow "bodies," as they are irreverently called, apparently because they are supposed to have no souls, who were going "doun the watter," as the phrase is, to their pleasant country quarters in the estuary of the Clyde, at Greenock, Gourock, Wemyss Bay, Rothesay, Dunoon, Kilmun, Strone, Tigh-na-Bruaich, and Ardrishaig. Some of the English travellers had arrayed themselves in the Highland costume, with the egregious Cockney idea, that the garb was customary on the mountains, and that it was obligatory upon any one who aspired to be considered a gentleman. Others, equally preposterous in their notions, had provided themselves with alpenstocks, as if there were a Mont Blanc or a Matterhorn and countless glaciers in Inverness-shire and Ross-shire, where such conveniences for clambering into or over dangerous crags and crevasses would be useful. And others, again, who would not on any account have made such fools of themselves in Piccadilly or Pall Mall, had donned the convenient knickerbocker suit, while they had rendered their lower limbs ridiculous by wearing a red stocking on one stalwart calf and a green one on the other.

One man, with a bundle of alpenstocks in one hand and a brace of fishing-rods in the other, had attired himself in a complete suit of pea-green; a pea-green hat, a pea-green feather, a pea-green coat and nether garments, pea-green hose, and, to be quite in keeping, pea-green boots. His appearance, of which he was evidently proud, procured him among the passengers the sobriquet of "the pea-green snob." He was a tall, handsome fellow, the observed of all observers; and doubtless mistook the mock admiration extorted by his fantastic garb, for real admiration excited by his good looks and comely proportions.

The succession of some of the grandest scenery in the world, that stretched in ever-varying magnificence all the way from Glasgow to Inverness, through the Estuary of the Clyde, the Kyles of Bute, Loch Fyne, the Crinan Canal, to the lovely rock-bound shores of the Island of Mull, within sight of Iona, Staffa, and the Treshnish Isles, by Kerrera to Oban, and from beautiful Oban to still wilder sublimities—to Ballahulish and Bannavie, and thence through the chain of glorious lakes, prosaically called the Caledonian Canal—has attracted the admiration of millions of travellers during the last half-century. The fairy region has often been described, but never yet had justice done to it by pen or pencil, and never will have; for words are weak, and art is tame, when the grander aspects of Nature have to be pourtrayed. The whole land is grand and beautiful, and as full of memories and traditions as it is of physical loveliness.

> " For over all the hazy realm is spread
> A halo of sad memories of the dead,
> Of mournful love tales ; of old tragedies
> Filling the heart with pity and the eyes
> With tears at bare remembrance ; and old songs
> Of love's endurance, love's despair, love's wrongs,
> And triumph o'er all obstacles at last,
> And all the grief and passion of the past.

There is no district of the same extent in any part of the known world, with which so many historical and legendary incidents of romantic and never-failing interest are associated ; and, as Dr. Johnson says of one of the most re-markable islands of the many that gem the Atlantic on the western shores of Scotland, the heart is cold and dead, the imagination torpid and insensible, that can pass among them, and can behold them, unmoved by the tenderest human sympathy.

" It will always be a matter of regret," said Mr. De Vere, " that Sir Walter Scott, when he made the circuit of Scotland in the steamboat of the Fishery Commissioners, did not sail up the Caledonian Canal, through the grand scenery of Loch Ness. What noble materials for a romance he might have found in the ruins of Urquhart Castle, on a projecting crag of the lovely lake ! "

" I forget the legends, if any, connected with it," replied Lady Stoney-Stratford, "and should be pleased to be reminded of them."

" In the first place," said Mr. De Vere, "the vaults of the castle are supposed to contain—deep buried in the earth—two great iron coffers, the same in size and in appearance, with not a mark or vestige to distinguish the one from the other, which have been concealed therein for centuries. They have been saved from the desecrating shovels of the ' Dry-as-dusts' of antiquarianism, and from the still more desecrating touch of the seeker for hidden gold, by the legend that one contains the ' Plague,' and the other an enormous amount of treasure in gold and silver and precious stones, and that if any mistake were made, and the wrong coffer were opened, so devastating a plague would overspread all Scotland—and even England—that the whole island would be depopulated."

"A fruitful idea for the genius of the 'great Wizard' to operate upon," said Lady Stoney-Stratford; "and more especially," she added, "if what was supposed to be the right coffer should have been found to contain, when opened, nothing but stones and rubble, or sand from the shores of the lake!"

"Yes, indeed," replied Mr. De Vere; and a splendid homily on the old story of the vanity of human wishes he would have made upon it. But of more value, and more novelty in his experienced hands, would have been the fact that Castle Urquhart was originally built and utilized by a colony of Knights Templars, or Knights of St. John of Jerusalem. The relations existing between these chivalrous soldiers of the Cross and the wild and lawless, but picturesque Highlanders, would have afforded him scope for a romance of more interest even than 'Rob Roy,' or the 'Talisman,' or any other of his matchless fictions."

The young ladies of the party, who, however, confessed to a better acquaintance with the writings of "Ouida," and Miss Braddon, and Marie Corelli, greater and purer than either of them, than with those of Sir Walter Scott, of which they knew something, though not very much—as they

14*

considered him to be no longer fashionable—agreed in Mr. De Vere's and their mother's opinion; and Lady Gwendoline even thought it an "awful pity" that Sir Walter had not penetrated the wilds of this "charming" region. How "dreadfully" dull it must have been for the Templars, who had a "sweetly beautiful" place of their own in "dear old London," somewhere in Fleet Street, in the very centre of fashionable society. "Poor creatures! But I suppose they hunted and fished, and stalked the deer on the mountains to amuse themselves?"

"Or chanted Latin hymns in the cloisters of the castle," said Lady Maud; "or made war against the wild cattle-stealers, that were the only inhabitants; or perhaps endeavoured to convert them to Christianity! They must have had plenty of society."

Mr. De Vere suddenly, if not impatiently, left the ladies to their prattle, and sought Mr. Rameses, who was seated alone at the further end of the steamer, drinking in with delight the manifold beauties of the gorgeous panorama of lake and mountain, watching the progress of a storm that was evidently impending. It burst at last, while they stood together, protected from the rain in the lee of the funnel, and enjoying the grandeur of the scene too intensely to seek shelter in the cabin below, whither the remainder of the company had made all haste to retire.

> " For lo ! the gusty rain with fitful whirl
> Beats in their faces, and the lightning flash,
> Illumines Heaven with glare blue venomous,
> And drags behind it, in its fiery car,
> The obedient thunder.   Lifting up its voice,
> It speaks to all the hills, which answer back."

" It is a strange and powerful fascination that the lightning has over my imagination," said Mr. Rameses; "and with what an eloquent voice the thunder seems to discourse to my soul, and hint, rather than proclaim, the profoundest secrets of mighty Mother Nature.   The old Asiatic belief, that is prevalent even in Europe, that thunder is the voice of God speaking in wrath to the wicked, and calling upon them to repent of the evil of their ways, does not appear to me to be superstitious, or to express anything else than the solemn truth.   God is always speaking to the wicked, if not by the thunder of His heavens, by the still small voice of conscience, heard alike in the wildest commotions of the elements and in the quietest repose of the mind.   I have often thought, though perhaps I may be wrong, that those who feel a coward fear in a thunderstorm, are self-condemned by the very fact of the abjectness of their terror!"

"I share your love of the storm," replied Mr. De Vere; "but not the reasoning which you build upon it; and while thoroughly agreeing with the great poet, that our philosophy is weak and limited, even in its wildest and widest flights, I hesitate to confound the merely personal cowardice of the weak and timid with the consciousness of guilt."

"The question is not to be discussed," replied Mr. Rameses, " though I strongly incline to the belief that more can be said for it than is likely to find favour in a mechanical and prosaic age; but what an instructive volume might be written, or perhaps has already been written, on the latent truths concealed in what a world of wiseacres considers to be the delusions of the vulgar! And what a hold many ideas which ultra-realists maintain to be superstitions have acquired over the mind and habits of some of the very wisest of mankind! Signs, portents and auguries are veritable powers in the government of the world, and have been so from the earliest ages of history and tradition. Rainbows and comets have been pressed into the service;

even the stars in their eternal sublimity have been degraded into fortune-telling diagrams and puzzles, and made to answer the purpose of riddles and conundrums. The idea of the voice of God speaking to the wicked in thunder, is a far nobler, and may be a truer, conception of the might and majesty of the Creator, than nine-tenths of the idle fancies that have hitherto led men astray, and filled them with false hopes or groundless terrors."

It was while indulging in such semi-philosophical discourse as this, that the two travellers and their less philosophical companions arrived at Inverness, where they were to pass the next day—unprepared for the gloomy monotony of a Scottish Sunday, but resolved, nevertheless, to make it a day of rest, as its Jewish name of the Sabbath proclaimed that it should be.

CHAPTER XXI.

PLATONIC ONLY.

A SOMEWHAT close though not intimate relationship had gradually established itself between the lovely and enthusiastic Laura de Vere, and the dreamy, calm, and philosophical Mr. Rameses. They were often thrown together while exploring the beautiful scenery of the Bens and glens, the streams and rivers, of the Highlands. They had many sympathies with each other, and they indulged in the same unfashionable and unpopular antipathies; and these very antipathies became links of sympathy. Miss De Vere had been strongly urged by the ladies of the Pierrepoint family to join them in fishing for trout and salmon in the lovely waters of the Spey, or in the broad expanse of Loch Awe, or Loch Etive, but she had a great repugnance to the sport, which she deemed to be cruel. So had Mr. Rameses. Both of them looked with the same repugnance upon the slaughter of grouse on the moors, and of ptarmigan on the crests of the mountains, and Miss De Vere was uncourtly enough to think that the Prince of Wales condescended to act the part of a poulterer's provider, or assistant, when he shot helpless doves by scores at a time in the preserves of Hurlingham, and looked upon the easy slaughter as an amusement. Mr. Rameses and the gentle Laura had nothing but animadversions to bestow upon what Mr. Rameses called the malicious patience and perseverance of the deer-stalking in which Mr. Fitzgerald and Lord Stoney-Stratford took such delight. The two had many other antipathies and dislikes in common, but in minor matters they differed but slightly—or agreed to differ—without preliminary consultation. Miss De Vere was of a practical, Mr. Rameses of a theoretical, tendency of mind; the one looked upon the world as it was, the other looked upon it as he imagined it ought to be; the one relied upon experience as a sure staff and support, the other upon hope as a guiding star.

And yet, with all their divergencies, each had a powerful attraction for the other, and were irresistibly drawn into companionship among the solitary wilds of the beautiful and romantic country in which their lot was temporarily cast. The scenery almost seemed to realise, in the mind of Mr. Rameses, his favourite idea of the twin-soul; one, yet divided; twin-forces, functions and intelligences working together, though they knew not how or wherefore, to the same ends. The twin-souls, about the vision of which he so dearly loved to speculate and to dream, were like two rivers that flowed into the same ocean; two eyes that looked with delight upon the same object; two hands that were engaged in the same labour; two feet that travelled on the same road; two lips that breathed the same word; the two breasts of a young mother that yielded the same nourishment to a beautiful infant; two nostrils partaking of the same odour, and two ears listening to the same divine melody.

Lady Stoney-Stratford noticed with disappointment, not to say displeasure, the growth and progress of a companionship that interfered more or less with the realisation of a project that she had formed in her own mind. Ever since the ill-omened marriage of Lady Gwendoline with Mr. Fitzgerald—for ill-omened, if not degrading to the house of Pierrepoint, she could not choose but consider it, in spite of her lord's personal and pecuniary reasons for looking favourably upon the alliance—she had cherished the hope that either Lady Maud or Lady Ethel would, with a little dexterous management on her part, win a place in the affections of the noble and wealthy Indian Nabob, and be led triumphantly to the altar, to share in the magnificent income of £150,000 per annum; a sum that would almost purchase the fee-simple of the Pierrepoint estates. The young ladies themselves were not so simple as not to suspect, and indeed to know, that such was the worthy woman's design in their interest, though each of them—though not caring very greatly about the matter—would have been better pleased if she, and not her sister, had been considered the magnet that was certain to attract to herself the as yet undecided fancy of the millionaire.

Had Lady Stoney-Stratford known all, and had she been in the confidence of her youngest daughter, she would have concentrated her anxieties upon Lady Ethel. But she knew nothing, and suspected nothing, of a possible *mesalliance*, more fearful than that which had been already consummated between the proud Lady Geraldine and the rich proprietor of the Methuselah pills. And it was well for her peace of mind that she did not, for her temporary ignorance was real bliss while it lasted. Lady Maud was the youngling of the flock, the only one among them that had a particle of romance in her composition. She was musical, literary, and unmercenary, unworldly, and scorned to turn up her pretty little nose at the idea of love in a cottage, which she thought was rather a good thing than a bad one—with all the greater cogency, perhaps, because her flowery destiny had never brought her within sight of it.

In the very worldly mind of Lady Stoney-Stratford, the doubt whether either of her daughters would consent to marry a good man, who, however good he might be, was not a Christian, was a source of constantly-recurring anxiety. In fact, the doubt, and the many difficulties that sprung from it, filled her otherwise tranquil existence with a trouble that she did not even confide to her husband, from the fear and almost the certainty that he would not sympathise with it. All his desire was to add barn to barn, acre to acre, field to field, domain to domain, that he might be the greatest landed proprietor in the county. For this darling object he had consented to waive his objections to an alliance with "Methuselah," as he delighted with grim jocosity to call his son-in-law; and for this object he would have waived his objections, were they thrice as great as they were, to an alliance with so great and wealthy a potentate as Mr. Rameses. And when his lady on rare occasions poured her doubts and fears into his inattentive ear, he gave the question the go-by with the easiest possible nonchalance, or with a passing suggestion that the faith of the Oriental magnifico might not sit very heavily on his conscience, and that if he made his home in England, as it seemed most probable he would do, he would conform to the ways of the country, and go to church on Sundays as regularly as other professing—but possibly not more real Christians than he was—were in the habit of doing. Lady Stoney-Stratford was partly of the same opinion, not understanding the deep earnestness of character, and the firmly-rooted faith of the Eastern philosopher, who had studied for himself the doctrines of all the ancient and modern religions that had hitherto found acceptance in the world. If Mr. Rameses would but conform outwardly to the faith of the English people, she did not consider his inward conformity to be of much or of any importance. And she thought that Lady Ethel would not be harder to please in this respect than she herself was, though she was not quite so sure of the sentiments of Lady Maud.

It happened one day that Lord Stoney-Stratford was confined to the house by an attack of his ancient enemy the gout, and was thereby unable to accompany Mr. Fitzgerald and Sir Henry de Glastonbury on a deer-stalking expedition in the forests of Monaliadh, or the Grey Mountains. The young ladies of the household had also been imprisoned in their rooms by a temporary tyrant quite as imperious as the gout—the tyrant Fashion, and its prime minister the Toilette—absolute ruler of the female world. Mr. Rameses found himself in consequence, though quite accidentally, alone for a full hour in the company of Lord and Lady Stoney-Stratford. The conversation was artfully, but delicately and diplomatically, led by Lady Stoney-Stratford to the subject of Christianity in India, and to the possibility of its extension among the Hindoo and Mahometan population. Neither Mr. Rameses nor Lord Stoney-Stratford had any great hopes that it would make any sensible progress for many generations, if it ever made any at all. "What can you expect?" said Mr. Rameses; "the religion of Mahomet, though that of the minority in India, appeals strongly to the passions of a pleasure-loving people, and promises the joys of a carnal and lascivious heaven to a carnal-minded and lascivious race, as the rewards of a short struggle with the cares and anxieties of a world that is but a dark and tearful world at the best. Brahminism and Buddhism, that were established long anterior to Christianity, have a firm hold upon the affections and prejudices of the people, and more than that, teach a doctrine near akin to, if not the same, as Christianism in all its essential points."

"How so?" said Lady Stoney-Stratford, to whom the statement seemed as new as it was startling.

"They both teach adoration and love of the Supreme Being, and the paramount duty of loving your neighbour as yourself. They also teach the immortality of the soul."

"But not the equality and brotherhood of all mankind," interrupted Lord Stoney-Stratford, "or the return of benefits for injuries, which lies at the very foundation of the Christian dogma."

"Do Christians themselves believe it?" answered Mr. Rameses. "Do they ever act, have they ever acted, on that divine principle? If they have done so, whence arise war and slavery, and the persecutions and martyrdoms of heretics? Whence come the insurrections and

the revolutions—the robberies—the spoliations—the mur-
ders and the assassinations—that have disgraced humanity
from the creation of the world downwards? Does a rich
Christian renounce his riches for equitable distribution
among the poor? Do Christians hold all the good things
of the world in common? Does the devoutest Christian
turn his second cheek to the smiter, after the first has
received the insulting blow?"

"I grant Christianity has not yet reached that high ideal,"
said the lady, "but it is travelling towards it, and will reach
it in God's appointed time."

"Meanwhile," said Lord Stoney-Stratford, "it has renounced idolatry, and believes but in one God, the
creator, the preserver, and the redeemer. It worships neither
images, nor even the heavenly bodies, as some nations do
and have done. The worship of the sun and the stars is
not even yet extinct in India."

"Pardon me," replied Mr. Rameses, "it is extinct, if the
word can be applied to that which never existed."

"Never existed," ejaculated Lord Stoney-Stratford, with
great surprise. "Not even among the disciples of
Zoroaster?"

"Not even among the disciples of Zoroaster—or the Parsees, my ancestors," replied Mr. Rameses, with unusual animation. "The Zoroastians never worshipped, never adored the Sun—never acknowledged him as God—but recognised him only as the sublime and beneficent manifestation of God's power and glory—the source of life and beauty—the upholder of the planetary system—which, but for his mighty and sustaining power, would be hurled into chaos. There needs no holy books—no Vedas—no Korans—no Bible of the Jews—no Evangel of the Christians—to prove to the world that, without the light and heat of the Sun, all life in the world would be impossible ; and the Zoroastians in acknowledging the fact, and being grateful for it, did not become idolators, and accept the shadow of the Divinity—which the Sun is—for the Divinity himself."

Lady Stoney-Stratford winced, as if in sore perplexity, and more than half inclined to relinquish all further controversy. Mr. Rameses—seeing her pain—came to the rescue. "I would not be misunderstood, my lady," he said, "or cause you even a moment's anxiety on my account. All things considered, I claim to be as good and true a Christian, in heart, as the Pope—or the Archbishop of Canterbury—or as any martyr that ever went to the stake to seal his faith with his blood. I acknowledge God, and worship him. I obey his laws as far as I am able, and love my fellow-man and my neighbour as myself."

" I have nothing more to argue about," said Lord Stoney-Stratford. " Nor I," added his wife. " The heart and the conscience are the guides, and, if they are satisfied, what right have we to make objections if the life be blameless ?"

Here the subject dropped, and would not have been renewed, even if the young ladies, having finished their devotions at the shrine of the great goddess, Fashion, had not entered at the moment, and rendered all further discussion inexpedient and improper.

Lady Stoney-Stratford afterwards made her daughters acquainted with the discourse that had been held with the Oriental philosopher, and both the young ladies agreed that Mr. Rameses could never expect that a Christian girl would marry him.

Lady Stoney-Stratford was convinced after this that her dream of an alliance of the Parsee with one of her daughters was at an end—and resigned herself to the inevitable, like a wise woman as she was.

Next day, Mr. Rameses, as if to prove to himself that his heart was in the right, and that he held his wealth in trust for the benefit of his suffering fellow creatures—signed cheques of large amount towards the support of every hospital in London. He did not even let his secretary know what he had done; and, moreover, imposed it as a command upon the several secretaries of the institutions which he had benefited, that his contributions should be only acknowledged in their archives as the benefactions of an anonymous donor. "This," he thought to himself, "may not be Christianity, nor love to God, but it may be love to man."

CHAPTER XXII

MR. RAMESES, with Mr. Melville, and Mr. De Vere and his fair daughter, were by no means sorry to leave the solitude of the Highland hills—for to them it appeared more than solitary for want of the congenial studies and occupations to which they were accustomed. The society and pursuits of Mr. Fitzgerald afforded them no inducements to prolong their stay. Mr. de Vere longed to be once again among his books, and Mr. Rameses among his Egyptian papyri and sarcophagi, and to be free of venal and vulgar companionship. While Mr. de Vere and his daughter made the best of their way to London, and Lord Stoney-Stratford remained on the moors—to slay grouse and deer—Mr. Rameses, accompanied by Mr. Melville, made a detour from Ross-shire and Inverness-shire into beautiful Perthshire, in order that the former might gratify a long-cherished desire to make his ascent of the noble Ben Ledi—that overlooks the village of Callander. To his mind the whole region was hallowed ground, trodden as it had been, during successive ages of what is called semi-barbarism —but as he thought of real piety and devotion—by millions of feet, who, on May mornings, or " Beltain 'Eens," of many recurring centuries, had made pilgrimages in long procession to the summit of this hill to kindle a fire—direct from the rays of the sun—between dawn and noon on that memorable anniversary.

Callander is now but a miserable village, but, to the mind of the Oriental philosopher, all the remembrances of the spot were sacred, not alone from their immense antiquity, but from their intimate associations with the earliest religion of the world—whether called Sabæanism, Sun-worship, or Fire-worship.   His secretary having, like himself, a strain of Asiatic blood in his veins, sympathised in a great degree in his love for the antediluvian faith of the earth's earliest fathers, and looked forward with curiosity and interest to the imposing ceremonial that Mr. Rameses proposed to perform on a magnificent scale.   His purpose was to draw fire from the direct rays of the sun, and to kindle a beacon that should light up the whole range of the Grampians, and the hoary summits of Ben Nevis, Schehallion, Cairngorm, and Ben Cruachan, and their gigantic brothers Ben Lomond, Ben Lawers, Ben Venue and Ben Goil. It was a fascinating idea to both of their minds, and associated with venerable and awe-inspiring traditions.

The fact that September had arrived, and that May morning was the orthodox anniversary of the Druidical celebration, did not cause Mr. Rameses to change his plan or diminish the interest with which he looked forward to its fulfilment. Mr. Rameses was particularly gratified to find on his arrival at Callander that the pilgrims of a long-past age had left their traces behind them upon the mountain, and that the broad pathway which their pious feet had trodden, from the base to the summit, was unmistakably marked by a broad belt of grass, amid the heather that fringed it upon either side. To a mind so richly stored as was that of Mr. Rameses, with the antique lore and traditions of the almost immeasurable past, it was not difficult to recall in fancy the long procession of Priests, Bards, and Prophets chanting in full accord their deep-voiced anthems to the Lord of Life and Light—and through him to the Great Creator, of whom, and of whose majesty, he was the most glorious reflection and representative on this poor ignorant Earth.

Filled with such thoughts as these, Mr. Rameses and his companion reached the summit of the Ben. Scarcely noticing, in their intense pre-occupation, the splendour of the landscape that gradually unfolded itself before them, they suddenly discovered that they were not alone on the hill, and noticed, with surprise and wonder, that, leaning with her arm upon the cairn that had been erected upon the summit, stood the graceful figure of a young woman, who seemed to be completely unconscious of their approach. She was clad in a long loose garment of pale amber, bound at the waist with a sash of golden fringe. On her head she wore, like a turban, a rose-coloured muslin cloth, twisted above her brow—but which allowed a few straggling locks of her raven-black hair to escape from the ligature that strove in vain to hide its abundant beauty. Her long dark eye-lashes concealed the brightness of the twin orbs, that were bent upon the ground, as if she were lost in deep thought and meditation. Her features were of an unmistakably Oriental cast, a pale brown, but beautiful tint, proclaiming her to be, as she undoubtedly was, a daughter of the East, whose ancestors had transmitted to her frame and face the colours of her clime. When she at last raised her eyes, and, with a slight exclamation of surprise, though not by any means of terror, became suddenly aware of the presence of strangers, Mr. Rameses thought he had never before beheld a vision of such transcendant oveliness as that which was suddenly disclosed to his sight.

When verbal intercourse had once been established between the three persons thus brought unexpectedly to-gether, it was soon ascertained that the fair and mysterious stranger had but a limited knowledge of the English language. Mr. Melville, who was an admirable linguist, endeavoured to come to the rescue by addressing the lady in Persian—but of this language she was ignorant. Mr. Rameses next addressed her in Hindustani, which he spoke perfectly, as did she also. By this means he learned that she was the sister of the Hindoo wife of a Scottish baronet, who had been engaged in some high administrative capacity in the service of a late Viceroy or Governor-General of India, and that she had come to Europe with her sister. She did not feel quite at home either in London, which was the usual residence of the family, and still less in the Highlands, where they had resided for the summer and autumn for the benefit of the mountain air, considered necessary for the failing health of the head of the family, who had drawn his first breath among the hills, and into whose debilitated frame every breath of the native elixir seemed to infuse new life and vigour. To this extent she was frank in answer to the questions that were politely but curiously put, and not pressed unduly upon her. In return for the information thus given she learned, to her evident pleasure, that both of her interlocutors were of Eastern birth and origin, and considered their accidental meeting to be of happy augury.

It happened—and the circumstance seemed to Mr. Rameses to be not only strangely sympathetic but highly propitious—that the object of the fair Oriental maiden, whose name was Niona, was like that of Mr. Rameses and his companion, to kindle a fire direct from the sun's rays, on the mountain top, in honour of the antique religion of Asia —if not of the whole world. Towards the accomplishment of this pious object, Niona, who had been on the summit from an early hour after dawn, had gathered together all the dry sprigs of heather and branches of gorse that she could find on the slopes. To these she had added such handfuls of the feathers of ptarmigan and grouse as she could collect —sole remnants of the feasts of the ravenous eagles, whose inaccessible eyries were on the neighbouring crags—until all these waifs and strays formed a respectable heap to aliment the expected blaze of the Beltain fire. But they were not sufficient for the mighty beacon that Mr. Rameses desired to enkindle. Mr. Melville was therefore deputed to forage among the lower levels and overhanging precipices, to gather bracken, roots of decayed heather, and, perchance, the scorched and lightning-smitten branches of larch, pine, and rowan, so as to build up a pyre worthy of such a great occasion as Mr. Rameses had imagined. His search was more successful than he had anticipated, and he reached the hill-top once again, suggesting to Mr. Rameses the pictures he had seen of the Man in the Moon, laden with sticks and faggots, which he bore in expiation of his supposed crime of Sabbath-breaking.

When the pyre had been duly constructed a little difficulty was experienced for want of paper to aid the effort of the fuel to burst into a flame. The difficulty was speedily surmounted by the production from the pockets of Mr. Melville of a quantity of letters and printed circulars, setting forth the merits of many proposed Limited Liability Companies, which had either been answered by the industrious private secretary, or required no answer. Mr. Rameses produced a powerful burning glass, and a handful of cotton wool. There was fortunately not a cloud in the clear blue sky, and, after a few minutes of patient expectation, during which the lovely Niona looked on with intense curiosity, the wished-for flame was produced—the dry twigs and bracken crackled merrily, the pine boughs yielded to the irresistible necessity that enveloped them, the blue smoke curled in beautiful wreathlets to the sky—and Niona knelt down devoutly in presence of the fire from Heaven. Mr. Rameses was scarcely less affected by the solemnity of the occasion—while on Mr. Melville devolved the self-imposed duty of keeping the straggling embers well together, and of feeding the flames with the, as yet, unconsumed branches and twigs that he had held in reserve.

The three lingered around the fire, and Niona—as if by a sudden and irrepressible impulse—broke out into a joyous chant, with a clear resonant voice of great power and sweetness. Neither of her companions understood the words of the song, though fully cognizant of its occult meaning. Gradually the jubilant and triumphant strain subdued itself into a soft lament, as the flames burned lower and lower, and finally dwindled into a melancholy moan and dirge, as the last spark flickered faintly and expired in the wood ashes.

The chant ended, Niona, without saying a word, turned slowly round and began the descent of the mountain. Her two companions followed silently and reverently down the grassy slope, without a word spoken on either side till they reached the entrance to the village.

" We part not thus," said Mr. Rameses, in Hindustani, "we must meet again in London."

" You will know where to find me," replied Niona, with a soft smile and a gentle wave of her hand, as she entered the villa of her sister's husband. And thus they parted. A deeper impression of the incidents was left upon the mind of Mr. Rameses than he would have deemed it possible that so casual a meeting, with one wholly unknown to him a day previously, could have produced even upon his imaginative nature.

CHAPTER XXIII.

Mr. Rameses, after his short and unsatisfactory wanderings in the Highlands—of which the only pleasant remembrance that he retained was his meeting with Niona—is again installed in his palatial residence in Kensington Palace Gardens. London was said to be empty, though there were only about four millions of people left in it—all nobodies in the estimation of the small circle of that which is called "Society," but each a somebody, and, perhaps, a great somebody, in his own. Mr. De Vere and his daughter had returned to the Rookery—Sir Henry and Lady De Glastonbury had gone home; the few philosophers, geologists, astronomers, Egyptologists and antiquaries, with whom Mr. Rameses had a personal acquaintance, had betaken themselves, some to America, some to the continent of Europe, some to the sylvan solitudes of the beautiful English shires, and some few to ducal or other aristocratic mansions—to figure as great lions among the smaller *feræ naturæ* of the fashionable world. After a fortnight's sojourn in the comparative seclusion of his Kensington home, Mr. Rameses had accepted the pressing invitation of his well-beloved friend, Mr. De Vere, to pass as short or as long a time as it pleased him in the Rookery, in companionship with the well-stocked library and museum of that pleasant abode—to muse, perhaps, upon the mysterious memories of Lurulà and Amenophra, and the splendid beauty of the living Niona—or to dream and speculate upon the seen and the unseen—upon Life, Time, and Eternity, and the boundless possibilities of the Infinitude. In these and kindred speculations, and in the congenial society of his friend, enlivened by the occasional society of his friend's daughter, the hours of Mr. Rameses—like those of Thalaba—"flowed pleasantly by," varied by occasional visits to the Metropolis, accompanied by his faithful secretary, for the transaction of his inevitable business—of which rich men have a fuller share than the poor, though the poor are often unaware of, and loth to acknowledge, the fact.

As the month of February approached, and the wandering English of the upper classes winged their flight from the remotest regions of the globe to the great central heart of

the world's business and pleasure, the thoughts of Mr.
Rameses turned towards the long-previously announced
succession of splendid dinners which, in an evil hour for his
peace of mind, he had consented to give. Though modest
in character, and frugal in his habits, he was not averse
from occasional displays of magnificent hospitality. He
was no lover of money for its own sake. He had no ideas
of hoarding it, and was pleased to possess it in superabundance—not alone for the good it enabled him to do,
and the well-being it was the means of diffusing, like sunshine and fertilizing rain, over a large surface—not for the
power over his fellow-creatures which it placed in his hands,
or for the sense of superiority, dear to the hearts of thousands of good people, who are not aware that they encourage
it. He was philosopher enough to feel that he could have
endured poverty without murmuring against the seemingly
hard Fate that yoked him to it—but also to know and to act
wisely upon the knowledge that wealth was good, when
employed to goodly purpose, and that the best of all rich
men were but trustees for the poor, and for the benefit of
those without whose labour it could not have been called
into profitable existence.

Preparatory to coming to any decision on the choice of the notable persons who should be asked to partake of the hospitalities which he intended to dispense on a princely scale, Mr. Rameses invited Mr. De Vere and his daughter to pass a fortnight with him in Kensington—partly that he might have the advice of Mr. De Vere, and partly that he migth enjoy the society of his daughter ; partly, also, that he might bring about an interview between them and the lovely Asiatic maiden whose acquaintance he had made on the summit of Ben Ledi.

He could not account for the fascination which, in spite of his will, the ideas of Amenophra, Lurulà, and Niona were linked in his mind by so many and such occult threads of sympathy, that he strove in vain to rend them asunder, and resigned himself to the dreamy hallucinations without any attempt to break loose from them. He did not confide his fancies to Mr. De Vere, or even to his private secretary, from whom he had few secrets—but hid them under his waistcoat, as the Spartan boys did the foxes—lest a too prying world should discover them, and sneer at his infatuation.

Mr. Rameses was one of those happily constituted men

"who are never less alone than when alone." The feasting on his own thoughts was a perpetual luxury. The dearest and most intimate companion of his thoughts was music— the music that his deft fingers drew from the great organ, on which he was an enthusiastic, though but little instructed, performer. Between the instrument and himself there seemed, in his own mind, to be a perfect sympathy. He talked to it—he played with it—he confided to it his hopes, his aspirations, his wildest fancies, and felt through all his frame the pulsation of electric waves, as the full, deep notes succeeded each other in unspoken hymns of praise, love, adoration, and exultation of spirit. He thought that the first music that sounded in the ears of human kind was heard by Eve as she walked in the gardens of Paradise and heard the Angels whisper together among the trees; that the music of the spheres was no idle dream of ancient or modern poets, but a physical and mental reality, audible to every human soul that was attuned to the all-pervading melodies and harmonies of Nature. Music, he said and thought, was a divine voice that was powerless to utter evil. It only spoke praise, love, adoration, cheerfulness, joy, and sympathetic exultation of mind. Discords might interrupt the concords that sounded from the seven strings of the lyre of Heaven—but they were alien, and antagonistic, and doomed to speedy extinction in the mighty diapason and full choral symphony of the Universe. Fear, Terror, and Wrath, might be imaginable in the sudden cessation of the harmony; but envy, scorn, malice, falsehood, jealousy, hatred, and all the ignoble passions and propensities of the perishing flesh, could find no voice in the angelic language of the spheres—in the voice of God, speaking from Eternity to Eternity—and regulating the march of suns, planets, and systems throughout the infinitude. Mr. Rameses found a sympathetic listener to his poetical rhapsodies on this subject in Laura De Vere—and in a lesser degree in the more prosaic, but still poetic, mind of her father. She was herself a performer on the instrument —and often attended on week days in the parish church of her native village, to make and enjoy a grander music than she could draw from the superb grand pianoforte which she possessed in her own home—and sometimes found her services in much request on the special occasions when the vicar, on the more solemn festivals of the Church, desired to impress the minds of his parishioners with a

holier rapture than that to which they were capable of being
lifted on more ordinary and frequently occurring occasions.
Mr. De Vere himself was of opinion—which he often expressed to the Vicar in friendly converse after dinner—that
the Protestant Churches of Europe, more especially the
Presbyterian and Calvinistic, ignorantly and perversely
neglected one of the noblest aids and incentives to devotion
when they banished all music except that of the untrained,
and too often harsh and discordant, voices of the congrega-
tion and the school-children, from their Sunday services.
"In fact," said Mr. Vere (and the Vicar in his heart agreed
with him, though he had not the courage to avow it too openly,
lest he should be suspected and accused of Ritualism, and
even of Roman Catholicism), " all the fine arts ought to be
pressed into the service of Religious worship—not only
music, but painting and sculpture; not only flowers, in-
cense, stained glass, drapery, but white embroidered robes
and flowing garments for the ministrants at the shrine and
the altar. Nor should the music of the organ and the
human voice, grand as these were, be confined," he
thought "to the service of the churches, but all, or more
than all, of the instruments in favour with Nebuchadnezzar

16*

which he commanded to be played in the service of Baal—the only God whom he recognised to be a God—(though Baal was only one of the names given to the Sun by the ancient natives of the East)—sackbut, psaltery, timbrel, harp, dulcimer, flute, lyre, and even the tabor and tambourine. All these were but the ministrants of sound, and sound was the gift of God, which, were it withheld from human ears, would render the earth uninhabitable." The Vicar, in the estimation of his principal parishioners, was thought to be somewhat wild and eccentric in his ideas on the subject, but all forbore to argue with him, for several reasons, the first of which was that no one among them felt himself quite able to controvert him, and was not disposed to enter upon so large a question.

It was decided by Mr. Rameses, who was warmly supported in the idea by Mr. De Vere, that to all of the grand dinners which he intended to give in the season, there should be a musical accompaniment—instrumental during the repast, and vocal during the dessert—when no clatter of knives and forks, the removal of dishes, or the passing to and fro of waiters, should distract attention from the sweet strains of the singers and choristers. Miss De Vere gladly undertook the management of all the details of this department of the festivals. She knew exactly where and to whom to apply both for instrumentalists and vocalists, and especially where she could obtain a well-trained choir of boys, whose voices she, with all other competent judges of music, held to be unsurpassable for clear and powerful melody. She also knew where to find most of the demi-goddesses of song, whose services were not monopolised by Paris, New York, Berlin and St. Petersburg—and who did not require a reward for administering to the enjoyment of an hour, as much as a year's wages of a dozen hard-working men.

Mr. De Vere recommended, if Mr. Rameses desired celebrity for his "symposia," that his guests should not be exclusively selected from the circle of fashionable life, but that they should consist of representatives of all the professionally intellectual classes, and should include—as opportunity served—patricians and plebeians, bishops and judges, generals and admirals, doctors and lawyers, authors and painters, bankers and merchants, and scientific philosophers of every class and kind—a perfect menagerie, in fact, of notabilities, more or less deserving of the eminence assigned to them in the small world that called itself, and was called "Society." But how to make a good choice amid such a multitude was the difficulty that beset both Mr. Rameses and his adviser. And then there were the ladies to be considered. But their claims Mr. De Vere thought might be easily disposed of by the invaluable aid of Lady Stoney-Stratford, and by garden parties in the beautiful grounds, and by balls in ˌthe splendid salons of the mansion. Thus, with dinners, concerts, garden parties and balls, the hospitalities of the rich Hindoo would indubitably become a nine days' wonder in the great metropolis, and sources of envy, ill-feeling, spite, and scandal on the part of all the non-invited who were above the social rank of shopkeepers. Mr. Rameses, in the face of the complications and hard work which he foresaw would be his lot in organizing these pretentious displays, was at times more than half disposed to abandon the idea of giving them. After all, as he thought, what would be the good of them ? beyond the spreading abroad of money that he did not value, to fill the greedy pockets of an extortionate crowd of harpies, who picked the pockets of the poor and committed wholesale robberies of the rich. But he had gone too far to retract. All the noble mothers of unmarried daughters in London were on the alert, with Lady Stoney-Stratford in the foreground, to turn this great occasion to advantage in the matrimonial market ; and, besides, even the philosophic giver of the festival had a vague notion, that he never expressed in words to anybody, that possibly, amid the crowd of beautiful women that would congregate around him on the occasion, the guiding-star of his life might be discoverable. The idea maintained its hold upon his mind, as he thought of Niona, the nearest approach to the bright "twin soul," that was seldom absent from his waking or dreaming fancy.

CHAPTER XXIV.

THE GRAND SYMPOSIUM.

THE advice given by Mr. De Vere was not exactly suited at the moment to the fancy of Mr. Rameses. The first of his series of dinners was not given to dukes, marquises, earls or bishops, but to philosophers and students of the wonders and mysteries of Nature. There was not a lord among the guests, except two, who were invited, not because they were lords, but because they were men who had sought Knowledge in her secret and remotest haunts, held communion with her, and given up their whole hearts to the fascination of her teaching—who had learned wisdom from the earth and from the stars, from the infinitely little as well as from the infinitely great. And these men were not staid and dull, and devoid of brilliant conversation—as the multitude are apt to suppose that men of high intellectual attainments too commonly are—but full of anecdote, wit, repartee and joyous elasticity. They were not expected to say good things, just as the flint and steel when quiescent are not expected to emit flashes of fire, but which never fail to emit them when properly handled.

Mr. Rameses was not only temperate but abstemious. His food consisted principally of grain and fruits, and his drink was water. He was by no means an anchorite or an ascetic in his hospitalities, but especially liberal in placing before his guests wines of the choicest vintages, in the excellence and virtues of which he was well initiated. He held—with the Apostle Paul, with Noah and Solomon, and with all the sages of ancient and modern times—that good wine was one of the choicest gifts bestowed upon mankind by all-bounteous, beneficent and benevolent Mother Nature. He was learned, and had been in his youthful time experienced, in the merits of Chateau Lafitte, Chateau Margaux, Clos Vougeot, Chambertin, Chateau Yquem, Romanée Conti, Marcobrunner, Rudesheimer, Tokay and Catawba, and was not to be imposed upon either by retail or wholesale merchants. He dealt directly with the vintagers and proprietors of Bordeaux, Burgundy and the Rhineland, and allowed the virtuous liquors to increase in virtue by age— for years after they had left the vines which gave them birth —and to mature in excellence as they matured in years.

And though, in this age of fads and isms, crazes and crotchets, the fact may be denied or not very cheerfully recognised, good wine is as powerful a magnet to attract good company, as good wit or the most sparkling conversation of the *beaux esprits* of society. The fame of the wine cellar of Mr. Rameses, the water drinker, was as widely extended as that of his wealth.

The accessories of a feast are better than the feast itself, or ought to be so. The coarse tastes of the palate are not the most refined of all the tastes that should administer to the luxurious charms of a sumptuous entertainment. The pleasures of the eye, of the olfactory nerves, of the touch, of the ear, and, more than all, of the imagination, are necessary to the completeness of the harmonies that should pervade every truly artistic banquet. The nectar of the gods would not taste like nectar if it were presented in a pipkin, and ambrosia would cease to be ambrosial if served from a coffee-pot. Who could sup Chateau Margaux with a spoon out of a soup-plate? Or Clos Vougeot out of a porridge pot? Plates of Sèvres and of Dresden ware add—though ravenously hungry and prosaic feeders may not be aware of it—to the flavour and zest of the delicacies that are provided in them; and the perfume of flowers, and the sweet strains of music, sounding amid the leaves and spreading branches of the choicest tropical palms and evergreens, enhance all the pleasures of sense, and prove with a somewhat different shade of meaning the wisdom of the words of Solomon when he declared, "that a dinner of herbs and love therewith" was better than the most sumptuous feast without that divine condiment. Silver and golden candelabra, cut glass, sparkling like diamonds, emeralds and rubies, and mirrors, reflecting a myriad lights, are all enhancements of the pleasure derivable from the gratification of the vulgar, and more or less degrading, appetite for mere food—which is the pabulum of the perishable body, but is no satisfaction to the imperishable mind, except in so far as in this purely physical world the mind is dependent upon the body for its power of communication with the material universe. Mr. Rameses had studied these things, and made use of his abundant riches to afford the fullest scope and play to his ideas.

All the great dinners that he gave during the season were social successes, and as such were duly recognised in the prevalent gossip of the time, blazoned abroad by all the usual organs of publicity—of which the tongues of the women, young and old, and of the quidnuncs of the clubs were not the least important. To the dinners were invited the leaders of the world of intellect and fashion—not without a *sotto voce* accompaniment of wonder that Mr. Rameses should give himself so much trouble about, and spend so much money upon, a world from which he expected and could obtain nothing in the way of advantage. But it was his whim, and had he not the means of indulging it? His hobby—and had he not the skill of riding it? But the success of the dinners, great as it was, was as nothing to be compared with the success of his garden parties. These were pronounced, by all the glibbest utterances of the great little world in which the utterers whirled about like lively animalculæ in a crystal vase, sparkling in the sunshine or the window of a drawing room—to·be the only events of the season that were worthy of remembrance— superior even in claims to the great annual Exhibition at South Kensington; that would be all very well in their estimation if the *oi polloi*, with their shillings, and the occupants of the Bath-chairs, wheeling about in everybody's way, were not admitted.

At these gatherings the beauty of all the beauties, whose loveliness was recognised by the men, and about whom the opinions of the ladies were divided into a small minority of admirers and a very large majority of dissentients from the popular verdict, was Niona Lal, who was accompanied by her sister, Lady MacTavish, and her sister's husband, Sir Hector MacTavish, knight of the Bath and of the Star of India. The next fair one who received the popular homage without claiming it, was Laura De Vere. The two young women were mutually attractive—the one fair as a summer morning, the other dusky, but beautiful as an autumnal evening, when the western sky is all aglow with many-tinted clouds, 'ere yet the moon has risen, or any other than the evening star·has put in an appearance in the sky. An idea spread abroad at these gatherings, from not one of which the dark beauty or the fair were ever absent, that Mr. Rameses, owing to the marked attentions which he showed to both of them, was like a moth hovering between two flames, uncertain in which of the two he should scorch his gauzy wings prior to the final immolation which the Ladies Pierrepoint thought to be inevitable. Lady Stoney-Stratford, however, was not without a faintly lingering hope

that the flames in the bright eyes of either Lady Ethel or
Lady Maud would yet prove of superior efficacy in attract-
ing the golden moth, although the young ladies themselves
had renounced all ideas upon the subject, and looked upon
the Paganism of Mr. Rameses as a fatal objection.   But
Lady Stoney-Stratford was a truly British General, and when
she thought herself likely to conquer never acknowledged
defeat or the possibility of it.   Besides, she knew that gold
was great, and that the " No," of a young lady might be
changed into " Yes," if pertinaciously ignored or contro-
verted.   Mr. Rameses, the person most interested, thought
no more of the supposed danger which he ran, than the
moth, with which he was ideally compared, thought of the
dangers of the blaze which dazzled and fascinated it.   The
lovely Niona was wholly unconscious of the fancies that had
taken root in the minds of the wealth-hunting English
maidens of aristocratic birth—but Laura De Vere, though
the most unmercenary of her sex, knew full well that Mr.
Rameses was not an utter stranger to the kindly and even
tender feeling with which she had almost unconsciously
inspired him.   She had no love of money, or of display—
her father was wealthy enough to provide liberally for all

her wants, whether she remained single, or found a husband in any station of life—and she would have hated herself if she could bave indulged in any scheme, or in any hope of an alliance with one whom she no doubt esteemed and respected, but for whom she had never entertained an affection of a nature different from that which she felt for her father.

Between her and Niona, with whom she had no thoughts of rivalry, the latent germ of a sisterly affection had gradually grown into an overshadowing tree. It had been to Laura a source of regret that she had no brother, and, above all, no sister who could sympathise in her joys, her sorrows, her studies and her amusements. She had unexpectedly found in Niona the friend, the companion, the sister she had dreamed of; and every day that they passed together served to increase the tenderness of the tie that bound them. Mr. De Vere watched the progress of the attachment with pleasurable solicitude, hoping that it might be strengthened as time wore on. Mr. Rameses also was a highly interested observer of the girlish love that had grown up in the sympathetic hearts of the two maidens—who had come into the world under such different circumstances, and been nurtured upon such different mental food. Greatly as he admired, and strongly as he was attracted towards, Laura De Vere, he more greatly admired, and was still more forcibly attracted by the inexplicable witchery exercised over his mind by Niona. "Blood," as has been often said, "is thicker than water," and the Asiatic blood that coursed through his own veins acted with a magnetic influence, which caused their pulses to throb in unison, when the thoughts of either of them turned towards the land of their birth—which became more than ever the land of their love, the further they were removed from it. The fancied resemblance·which Niona bore to the image he had formed in his mind of the long-lost priestess of Isis—the beloved Lurulà of his dreams—drew his sympathies more and more towards her, and withdrew them in a corresponding degree from Laura De Vere, who, on her part, gradually ceased to be conscious of exercising any greater influence upon his mind than that of the mild and equable influence of friendly sympathy and intellectual companionship.

Lady MacTavish was not happy in her married life, and

Niona partook, as she could not fail to do, of the discomfort of her position. Sir Hector was a specimen and a remnant—perhaps the last—of the old Highland gentleman of a bygone era. He had all the arbitrary notions of a feudal chief, longed for the restoration of the ancient privilege of pit and gallows, to be exercised at will against his refractory vassals, and treated his docile spouse after the fashion of the Eastern potentates, who looked upon women as chattels or toys, slaves to their will, and bound to render unresisting and uncomplaining obedience to their slightest caprices. In daily intercourse with such a tyrant—to whom she was only bound by the sisterly, or half-sisterly, tie of relationship—it was not to be wondered at that Niona should look with pleasure and favour upon the graceful courtesy, the delicate attention, the deferential respect exhibited towards her by one of her own race, who had discarded the Asiatic notions of women, and moulded his thoughts, his character, and his conduct upon those of Europeans towards the female sex. Mr. Rameses was in his whole mind, bearing and behaviour, a thorough English gentleman, of what is improperly called the old school—but which is neither new nor old—but perennial and perpetual, and likely to remain so. Under these circumstances, so novel in the experience of the fair Niona, the intimacy between her and Mr. Rameses grew more cordial as the days wore on, and gave additional strength to the rumours which floated about in Society, that all the wiles and snares and delicate manœuvres employed by the match-making mothers and match-desiring daughters of the fashionable world, who had set their hearts upon sharing the comfortable millions of Mr. Rameses, were likely to be exerted in vain, unless a change should come over the minds of either of the two interesting Indians— a change which, to lynx-eyed observers, did not seem possible on the lady's part, or probable on that of the gentleman's. And consequently, the secret war against the rupees of the millionaire languished a little, though it did not cease in the higher circles of the aristocracy. But Lady Stoney-Stratford remained alert and watchful— reposed a little, but did not shut her eyes against the chances and possibilities of the future.

 END OF VOLUME I.

www.ingramcontent.com/pod-product-compliance
Lightning Source LLC
Chambersburg PA
CBHW020357030726
47496CB00007B/2178